KNOWING THE ENEMY

THE LAST TRIBES OF BRITANNIA

LEA MORAN

CONTENTS

ACKNOWLEDGEMENTS

There are several people I must thank for reaching the end of this first published work:

My mother, Susan, for her endless patience in teaching me the difference between a sentence and a paragraph so late in life, not to mention the fine tuning of my random punctuation.

My sister, Sarah, for being the most creative and unceasingly positive influence.

All at Crowan Book Club for opening my eyes to good writing.

My incredible neighbours Andy, Anna, Maxine, Vicky and the dearly missed Alison, who critiqued the story at various raw and perhaps painful stages.

Also, to James, Meg and friends at Meneage Archaeology Group for bringing me the physical touch of history.

My three sons (essential sounding boards) Brendan, Aidan and especially Finlay for making my 5-minute stories into films for YouTube.

And Seamus, my husband, and for always understanding and filling the deep holes in my confidence.

Fictional map with approximate borders.

Historical note from the author can be found at the end.

The tribes of Britannia emerge from the abandonment of Rome to face the Angles, Saxons and Jutes settling from the east and encroaching on their territories. Over 100 years of battles, peace treaties, and payments of tribute have left a trail of switched allegiances, betrayals, and fear.

The ordinary folk continue the struggle to survive from the land but, inevitably, some are caught up in the tides of change and the whims of kings.

PROLOGUE

A.D.552

THE BANKS OF THE RIVER SABRINA
THE LAND OF THE DOBUNNI, A TRIBE OF BRITANNIA

My brother is up to his thighs in soft silt. Dirt flicks up to his hair as he struggles. I touch the cold place around my ruined ear where mine no longer grows. Then my cheek, the puckered scars of healed burned skin that pulls my mouth into a permanent lopsided grin.

'Luca!' Kennan spits grit. 'You will not be smiling when I get out of this and wrap my hands round your throat.' He, of all people, should be used to my distorted face.

'You have sunk too far, brother. You will not get free. Even the curlews and dunlins avoid these sink spots.'

We both glance at the tiny imprints of birds' feet that criss-cross the nearby mud, while the wet circle that traps him gleams smooth in the sun. The signs are there, yet still he launched himself in.

'I will get free, just you wait.' He slaps hard at the mud. 'The tide still has a long journey out to the sea. It'll be hours before it comes back in.'

The receding tide has already revealed the wide brown plains of the river bend. 'And when it does, you know as well as I, it will slowly creep up to that weed line but then it will race, churning up the silt, rolling and swallowing everything in its path.' I picture the moment with satisfaction.

'I am not worried about that.' He juts out his chin as he shouts. 'I will be long gone by then.'

1

'By even-time, the river will be a bright reflection of sky. And you will be a memory beneath.'

'Maybe it will be your sorry carcass that will be under the water.'

He will not admit he is in peril but he writhes like a landed eel. Each effort to raise one leg drives the other further down. He will sink deeper but I am unmoved. The smell of mud settles at the back of my throat but it is the sour tang of death that lingers on my tongue.

Stones press through the worn ox-hide of my boot soles. My legs are weary from the running of the last two days. I step back from the shore and sit down on a boulder. A blackbird sings from the rowan tree behind and I am reminded of our mother. The guilt of a promise twists within me. For her, I will consider saving him. If I think back, perhaps I will find a reason to do so. Every last incident leads me to the one before, and the one before that; a bow string pulled tighter and tighter, now the arrow is loosed and the consequences uncertain. I will have to go back a long way, even to the beginning.

Well, Kennan is right about one thing, the tide will not turn for a while.

1

I have our father's name of Lucanus, shortened to Luca. My brother has his looks and his love. I was born in the tail's tip of the year 534 when snow veiled the solstice sun, and so the passing of my life is measured in winters. Kennan was born just a year and a season later as the blackthorn trees bloomed white. My earliest memory is our father holding Kennan up and swinging him around, calling him his *miracle*. I hugged his leg, hoping for the same but he prised me away. Mother drew me into the warm folds of her gown as she cradled our sister, and my cheek brushed against her sweet baby head.

When I picture Minura, it is with barefoot and tawny curls toddling across the yard with the geese. I mimicked her to make her giggle and she batted her hand at me, saying, '*Stop it, Luca,*' her voice like the chatter of sparrows. Though Kennan made her laugh too, there was a sparkle in her eye she saved only for me.

My memories of those early days are accompanied by the sensation of Kennan's shoulder nudging against mine; running together or sat with his arm flopped over me as he whispered in my ear. The world fell out of balance when the heat of him was not at my side. Play wrestling was common. He laughed as we lay on our backs, rubbing bruised limbs, though there were times I would lick blood from my teeth before forcing a grin.

Lucanus is the potter of Framlutum. He sits on the Market Traders' Council in Glevum, the major town nine miles away, and is the man who brings news from the world beyond into the small sphere of our village. His pottery was not a place for small children.

3

Boarded on three sides and roofed with leaky sedge thatch, I loved to sit watching him work but Kennan fidgeted beside me.

Though Father was stern, the infectious laughter of my brother could bring out a merrier side. When he needed clay, he took us to the shallow pits just over a mile away. 'Come, mochyn,' he would say, using the old word for pig and lifting us onto the rough boards of the empty cart. We sat clinging to each other as the wheel rode its familiar rutted groove through the woods, laughing as he bounced us up over gnarled roots. He pretended to overbalance crossing the stream over a well-worn plank, making us squeal, then steered wildly between gorse bushes so we'd cry out and snatch up our bare legs from the prickles.

Traversing the eerie wetland over more planks, he slowed and his eyebrows drew together once more. I clung to the edge. Kennan still wriggled in silliness.

'It's the clay makes it so wet,' Father explained the first time. 'It traps the water. Feel it.'

The soft clay slipped between my toes as I stepped into the shallows and goose-bumps prickled up my legs. The clouds above glinting silver in the pool, I stared at my reflection. My black hair was different to the moth-brown of my brother and father, my pale narrow face had not the ruddy round cheeks of theirs. My eyes held no lively glint like my brother's. No wonder our father favoured him. My image wavered and broke apart as I sunk my fingers in.

Father had a shovel and we each had a trowel fashioned from a sheep shoulder blade. We dug. Trowelful by trowelful, we loaded clay onto the boards of the cart as the brown water ran away through the gaps.

'Pile it on. It will dry out and stick. Form a mound in the middle, like this.' Father dumped his shovelful, a mountain compared to our efforts. I carefully heaped clay onto my trowel each time, placing it as Father said. Kennan slopped lumps and muddy water all over.

Cold clay flicked over me. Jumping back, I fell with a splash. Kennan laughed, as did our father, so I laughed too. I flicked cold water at Kennan and a playful tussle began until we were both lagged in clay. It ended as Father's fat fingers pressed roughly into my arm. 'Enough! Twp mochyn!' *Idiot pigs.*

We followed his feet and the rumble of the cart homewards, our britches sticking to our thighs as we walked, clay drying into our hair and the creases of our skin. My buttock stung from a trowel-slap: I was the oldest, I should have known better.

**

While Lucanus was important in our remote village, my mother was from a high-status family in Glevum. Her father was Atto, chief steward to King Aurelius, ruler of all the Dobunni lands. She had grown up under the shadows of *'the purple'*, the colour of royalty Aurelius liked to continue from the old days of Empire. No-one else in our village had ever met the king and Father bristled when she spoke of her past.

I longed for her tales of court life. Curled up on the straw mattress, Kennan and Minura already asleep, I begged her, 'Tell me a tale of the king.'

'Alright, my lamb.' She smiled and settled in against me as shadows of thatch danced in the flickering lamplight. 'What shall it be?'

'Tell me again about the king's hair.'

'Well, after a skirmish with the Jutes it turned white overnight,' she whispered into the quiet of the roundhouse as the daubed walls sucked away other sounds. 'Not long after, the hair on top of his head fell out, bald as a baby bird.' I imagined the old king. 'He tried every potion to grow it back but his white beard grew longer and longer.' She laughed. 'So long, that it once caught in his buckle and no-one dared tell him.'

'Why not?'

'His foul temper! He often punished a servant for the wrongs of another to keep order. Even the courtiers and chieftains trod carefully before him. But Atto understood the nature of Aurelius. He told me the king has fears like everyone else.'

'What does the king fear?'

'The *Jutes*, of course. Cynric Claw-hand hounds Aurelius. This brittle peace we have lived through cannot last.'

'Will Cynric Claw-hand take our land?'

'He might try. He has made an alliance with the *Saxons* of the Gewisse. Much has worsened since your grandfather's time.'

'Tell me about Atto.'

Her voice softened, her breath warm. 'He was always to be found at the right hand of the king, rushing to intervene in every dispute. Many say our king has become cruel and divisive, but in the days he had Atto…' She trailed off and Kennan rolled heavily over me to fill the warm chink between us. I made room for him.

I took my place in Kennan's shadow and was comfortable there. The beatings from Lucanus made me uncertain, while his praise made Kennan bold. Though we were different in character, we had much in common. We both liked the salty rind of the ham hock, and licking the smeared edge of the empty honey pot. We both loathed the musty scent of scratchy wet britches. Worst of all was Mother's cabbage soup; sitting side by side with legs crossed, we groaned in harmony and wrinkled our noses as we ate it. I was only happy when Kennan was happy with me.

Mother nurtured our bonds. Lucanus drove in wedges. She might try to soften his mood but only once challenged him directly. I was seven. Tears dried tight on my cheeks as I lingered alone in the yard. Mother had cooked a bean broth knowing the waft of it would draw me inside.

'Sit, Luca, my lamb.' She indicated the space between Kennan and Minura and scooped steaming food into a bowl for me. I sat down but tender bruising of a recent thrashing made me stand up. She looked across at Lucanus, his broad back to us all. I gulped a spoonful of beans, soft and thick in my mouth, calming me as I swallowed. After the meal we were sent out to play. Catching me as I went, she held me, her chin on my head. She let out a sigh so deep her breath ruffled my hair.

Playing in the yard, I heard voices raised in disagreement. Tugging at Kennan, I nodded toward the roundhouse. Leaning into the doorpost, pressed tight together, we listened.

'He's not going,' Father said.

'But Luca is seven winters now. I've arranged it with the monk.' Mother's words were unforgettable: spiked and hard like jagged rocks.

'No good will come of it. That old zealot Father Faustus is no stranger to trouble.'

'He's a man of God and is reconciled with his past. He's loyal to King Aurelius and well-learned.'

'What use is the learning? Luca must do his share of the work here.'

'The monastery is close enough! He can go when his chores are done and still be back for his bed.'

'It's not—'

'*Lucanus.*' She cut right across him. 'The king made me a *promise*, in gratitude for my family's loyalty. Though it seems *you* have forgotten the agreement, King *Aurelius* will honour it.'

'I forget nothing.' My ear to the doorpost was hot. '...But it is not fair...' I sensed the air move, his step across the floor. His words were spat and harder to hear. Kennan pushed heavily against me, eager as I. '...that Luca will go but Kennan will not have the same chance.'

There was a pause.

'When we married you wanted a child, a son to be the potter after you, or a daughter to care for you in your old age. Well, have I not given you both?' She was not giving up. 'Kennan will follow your path. But Luca will follow his own. He must go to the monastery to learn the writing… And you will let him.'

To my amazement, Father said no more. Kennan stepped away leaving the cold at my side. His mouth was shut tight. He was just six and probably understood less about the conversation than I, but Father's resentment that I was to learn at the monastery and he was not was clear to us both, and sparked the first tension between us.

2

'Luca! Come here.'

I leapt to Mother's side, a shiver of the evening air on my spine.

'In three days, you will go to the monastery. You will spend the afternoons learning the letters and marks of the scripts. My lamb, you must work hard and learn well.'

'But… Won't the monks turn me away?'

'Father Faustus will be expecting you.'

'And… Kennan?' I dreaded the division that must surely come.

'Just you.'

'Kennan will go too, when *he* is seven?'

'No, Luca.' She grasped my elbow and held me firm. 'When my father died, I had no status or guardian.' Her seriousness cast my fears about Kennan aside, I wanted only to make her happy again. 'The king could have turned me out but, out of love for Atto, he took an interest in my fate and allowed me to stay and serve the lady.'

'I thought you came here to Framlutum when Grandfather died?'

'Not right away… I met Lucanus and the king agreed to our marriage. In truth, he was relieved to be rid of me…' She averted her eyes. 'I was an untidy loose end to a difficult time, a reminder of bad days.'

'What bad days? It makes you sad. Why are you sad?' I leaned in against her; she smelled of apples and barley. It was easier to listen without having to see the pain of her memories.

'When my father died the world turned upside down.' She pulled me by the shoulders to face her. 'I'm not sad anymore. Not now I have *you*. In the end it all happened so fast; one day I was called before the king, the next day I was married, and the day after that I came here. *But* before I left the king made a promise. In honour of Atto, he promised that if I had a son he would learn to read and write – that's *you*, my first born. I have *ensured* the promise is kept. You must not let me down...'

'I will try, Mother. I will.' The thought of the monastery filled me with fear. She must have seen it.

'Perhaps,' she squeezed me tight, 'you will be a great man like your grandfather. Maybe serving the king as he did.'

As if to make a point, Lucanus found me many jobs to do. The thorn-fenced pens for the fattening pigs always needed repair, and the relentless driving back of elder and bramble in our three field strips behind. My first day at the monastery, I rose early to avoid him. After tending the hens and the pig as I usually did, I ran all the way.

Our small village of Framlutum lies between the great River Sabrina on one side and the high scarp hill on the other. Cattle roam in the lowland and among the ring of houses there is a continuous grey line rising from the smoke-house. The pale roof of the grain store catches the morning sun. Grazing in its shade are two ponies tethered to the communal cart. The monastery is in the next dale two miles away, on the site of an old abandoned villa.

I followed a new flinty wall to a door guarded by high-nesting rooks, cawing and squawking at my arrival. Thinking of the gossiped tales of hermits, saints, and relics, I pulled the bell-cord and waited as it chimed a doleful note. I shivered in the cold shadow of the door before me. As it opened, a bald old man greeted me, thin as a birch tree with fingers like twigs.

'God's greeting, boy. You must be Luca, I am Father Faustus.' I'd heard stories of the monk's temper but his face softened as he smiled. 'I am the keeper of the books.' There was another lad there, lanky and awkward with rough chopped hair. 'Luca, this is Crab, a novice. Crab, this is Luca.'

'Hello,' I said, but he did not meet my eye and scuttled off, one shoulder higher than the other, one leg dragging behind. His hair was shaved at the back and I could not take my eyes from him.

'Don't expect Crab to answer, he's *mutus*. But clever in his way and suited to this life... Our chapel is newly repaired,' he said, changing the subject and pulling me with him. 'Stone reused from the old villa.'

He led me past the crumbling ruins, new timber huts and neat rows of vegetables, to the chapel. Four pillars held a triangular top, decorated with a hunter-god and strange animals. I stood at the worn step, uncertain about going inside. The ancient walls were as thick as the span of my arms. 'These places must've been built by Hercules, or were all the men of that time giants?'

'Ah, so you know your stories! Good, good. I'll show you the ones we have written here and you'll learn to read for yourself. But first, we must work on the Latin.'

'Latin?'

'Yes, the Latin in the writing is pure and… precise. The way we speak is… different. You will know more Latin than you think. We mix it with words of a… local nature.'

I stepped inside. My breath froze in my throat.

'This was a temple to the *old* gods,' Father Faustus indicated to the mosaic of a bare-breasted Venus surrounded by intertwining lines, 'but is now dedicated to Christ. See the new Chi-Rho symbols?' The wall curved around at the end, with newly painted marks either side of an altar stone.

On the stone sat a small jewel-encrusted gold casket with a plain wooden cross set upon it. I reached out to touch the gleaming gold, he gripped my arm and firmly steered me away.

'Books and scrolls are the real treasures here.' His pale eyes narrowed with pride. 'The monks have collected them from many places.' He tightened the rope around his oversized robe and led me to a timber chamber at the side, dedicated to the care of the books and a place for further writings.

Father Faustus spoke other languages and read me script from the biblical world. He was passionate and free with his opinions, many of which I did not understand.

'God has sent the foreign wolves as a punishment for this sinful generation of backsliders and miscreants. Our future is doomed – failure in battle, our people taken as slaves to the heathen devils…'

'You mean the Jutes and Saxons?'

'Don't say those words! It is sacrilege to utter them here in the sanctum of our Lord! Victory and deliverance from our oppressors will only be won with divine intervention from God. And divine intervention will only be attained through purity of heart and…'

He would go on with this theme until distracted, which I soon learned to do. 'Is it true you once had to flee for your life?'

'Hmm, yes. A particular king took a dislike to my sermons… He's now dead and burning in hell for his sins… But God will…'

'So, will I really learn to read… and even to write?'

'Hmm? Yes, yes, there was once a time, you know, when all sons of the villas would be taught how to read. These days it is more often fatherless boys who are sent to me.'

'I'm not fatherless! But my father is only a potter.'

'But your grandfather was *Atto*. He was important. I never met him, but I heard he encouraged Aurelius to send others to be educated. Perhaps that is why the king has sent you to me.' He leaned in. 'Aurelius is sly, a *pardus*, an admirer of…'

'A *pardus*?'

'A leopard. You don't know?' He looked down his nose at me. 'Well, there are things you'll learn but all in good time… I was saying, Aurelius is an admirer of the greatness of the Roman legacy and likes to surround himself with clever men. He'll no doubt claim some use from you in the future, call in the debt he'll expect repaid. He may be wicked but he's not a fool.'

I found the reading hard but I liked Father Faustus. He traced the inky lettering with his leathery fingertip, tapping as he hinted at the clues they contained. My concentration slipped over psalms but became alert to the myths and legends of the Greeks and Romans. In the retreat of the monastery, I learned much of the wider world.

On my way home that first day, I glanced up at the knoll by the old oak and I saw a fine warrior – a distant but vivid splash of colour against the drab hillside. His white stallion with red tasselled bridle stood gracefully poised and still. The red cloak of the rider fluttered on the breeze as he raised an arm and waved. I looked around thinking someone else must be near, but I was alone, so raised my own arm in reply. Too late, the Red Horseman was gone.

When I imagined myself in the future, that is how I wanted to be. A man of importance like my grandfather, riding a magnificent steed. I kept the thought locked inside, my own private hope. The image returned to me in the dark of many nights and, even now, comes to my mind as alive as at that moment.

**

Kennan sulked. He did not ask about the severe old monk who had been in trouble with kings. He did not ask about the monastery. He did not ask about the mysteries of ink and parchment. So I said nothing. But each time I returned home the distance from Kennan caused a writhing in my belly. Eventually, his curiosity got the better of him and he began to ask questions, pretending he was not really interested. I hid my relief and answered, pretending I was not either. If he became prickly, I became silent. As the summer rolled into winter, the familiar warmth from his shoulder rubbing against mine returned and the tensions between us eased – for a while.

'Luca!' Lucanus growled my name as he warmed himself by the fire. I stood up, believing I was in trouble. 'Luca, the year is turning and you will be eight. My father began my training in the pottery at that age and I will begin yours.'

'And me, Father?' Kennan jumped up, excited.

'Not you.' Kennan's head dropped, dejected. 'Not yet.' Lucanus ruffled his soft hair, a gesture of kindness I had never once felt.

Lucanus was used to working alone. He grumbled whenever I touched anything. He gave detailed explanations, saying, 'Just as *my* father showed *me…*' but forgetting how it is to learn. I watched him beat the clay and tried to copy his every movement.

'Look closely, mochyn.' He began to work gently, creating a delicate shape, his frown deepening in concentration. 'Feel the clay and guide it. Now, you make something. Anything. And stay out of the way.'

I sat at a trestle table, a draught on my back from the loosely boarded walls. Tiptoeing to the wet-clay barrel, I pulled out handfuls and began to make creatures for my mother. She loved the birds, so I made her a little wren, a plump dove, and an elegant jay – her favourite. Father tossed them back into the barrel, but Mother kept the jay on a dark shelf. When it dried and crumbled, she swept it up, wiping her cheek as she threw the remnants outside.

Lucanus grudgingly accepted my emerging usefulness. Kennan grudgingly shrugged off his sulk. Though I had less time for play, I sought out his boisterous laughter and was even pleased to be wrestling and tumbling. Rubbing my bruises and licking blood from my teeth again, I would smile.

Another year passed and Kennan turned eight.

Having been itching for his turn in the pottery so long, his excitement ruffled feathers from the start. To demonstrate the need for obedience, Father swiped a hard back-hand to my head. He was holding a small shaping tool, and as I pressed my ear, the hot slip of blood warmed my fingers. Kennan, oblivious, was launching his arms deep into the wet clay barrel.

'Wait, lad, you'll have the barrel over!' Father followed him with a damp rag as he smeared clay over the table and stool. 'Don't go near the new pots, they're still soft and easily damaged.' He steered Kennan away, instructing him to spread the slippery clay onto dry boards to firm it for working with later. He droned on with lengthy details interrupted with, 'Don't touch that… Stop, listen now… Stay away from the pots.'

Father gave Kennan a wedge of prepared clay. 'Kneed it like this.' He showed him, pressing and rolling. 'Pick out any bits of leaves and twigs you find as you go.'

Kennan squeezed the clay through his fingers into pieces that fell to the ground. I noticed a twitch below Father's left eye. 'Like this,' I whispered to Kennan, working the smooth lump of my own. He frowned at me and collected the pieces of clay off the floor.

'No bits.' Father snatched his clay and threw it into the trees beyond. 'It'll be a bad firing if it's dirty.' He gave him another lump. Kennan soon became bored and returned to the pots drying behind him.

'Will I make pots like these, Father?'

'You'll learn the way of the clay first. *Don't touch them, boy!*'

Instead, Kennan reached over for the fine carved-antler shapers and scrapers. Our father tugged at his beard. A beating was brewing. Kennan had never known the sting of his hand or the bite of his stick. It would be me that got the blame.

Kennan knocked his board off the bench. It landed at his feet and he jolted back into the rack of fresh pots. The pots hit the ground.

Lucanus roared. Kennan was as white as the statues in Glevum. Lucanus grabbed him by one arm. Lifted him crying, lopsided and flailing, out to the yard.

'No, Father. Please, Father,' he whimpered.

I was as shocked as he was. I had already learned that begging and pleading only hardened Lucanus' wrath. There was nothing I could do. When the thrashing was done, he curled up, sobbing. I crouched right beside him but he pushed me away. The lively gleam in his eyes replaced with resentment.

'Go *away*,' he hissed. And I did.

3

I wanted Lucanus' attention, but it came at such a price. Working meticulously, my skill grew in forming fine things from the clay and, for the first time, Kennan was on the outside. When he felt the heat of Father's irritation, he knocked into my arm or kicked at my shin. I did nothing but suppress a tearful ache of guilt at the surprising reversal of our positions. But this only occurred in the pottery, as if the loose boards of the walls contained a new spell. Outside, Lucanus still blamed me for everything and after a while Kennan and I rubbed along well enough – when avoiding any talk of *monks* or *pots*.

When I was ten winters, a new focus arrived in our lives, one which would remain as an undercurrent to everything else. Father had been at the Market Traders' Council in Glevum and returned with the latest news of our king. My mother's stories were the past, Lucanus brought the future.

'King Aurelius,' he paused for dramatic effect and leaned forward, 'is after the missing relic of St Alban the Martyr.'

We all edged closer, wondering what he was talking about.

'It's said, God will give victory to whoever carries the relic into battle.' He pulled little Minura onto his lap. 'But it has been lost since the glorious days of Ambrosius.'

'Does he hope it will give us divine intervention?' An expression I learned from Father Faustus.

'Hmph.' Lucanus cocked his head and looked at me as if I had stolen his gold. 'The story goes,' he said, turning back to the others, 'that the relic was stitched into a silken strip Ambrosius wore across his heart. This gave him God's protection. But it's more than a lifetime since it was lost. Nothing but failures and losses have followed.'

'If Aurelius has it,' Kennan jumped in excitedly, 'he'll bring us victory over the Jutes and Saxons, and maybe the end of Cynric Claw-hand for good. Will you search for it, Father?'

'Me? No, I'll leave that to the men of Aurelius' guard.'

Kennan looked disappointed. 'Whoever finds it will be a great hero of the Dobunni.'

'For a thing that has been lost so long,' Mother said, 'how will they even know where to look?'

'The search is to start in Dumnonia. In an old fort where the land meets the sea, a place called *Din Tagel*, where some say Ambrosius lived his last days.'

There was a quiet among us. None of us had ever been further than the Dobunni borderlands.

'What *is* the missing relic?' I asked.

Lucanus did not answer.

Then Kennan asked and he replied. 'It's a finger.'

'His finger?' asked Kennan, looking at his own.

'St Alban was a man of the Calchwynedd, murdered for refusing to deny God. They say his blood still marks the ground.'

'But he is missing a finger,' I said.

'They say, it's wrapped in a fragment of his blood-stained tunic, perhaps still stitched into this silken strip. Who knows?' Lucanus got up. He had no more to say.

I wanted to know more.

I went to Father Faustus. Without hesitation, the old monk told me the story with passion and gilded references to God at every turn in the tale. I was keen to retell it in my own way among friends. My learning at the monastery had brought me new confidence and my quiet nature had begun to find a voice. Our friends loved the stories I told and many of our games grew out of them.

We met at the Glenring, a circle of mossy stones in the alder woods where the youth of Framlutum always gathered, a place we replayed battles, set ambushes, and captured enemies. A fallen tree became a ship sailing the high seas, a hollow oak was a fortress under siege, a long branch bridged a deep gorge that only the most sure-footed could cross. But that evening, our talk centred on the relic with the power to bring victory. With the cold at our backs, we made a fire.

'So, the Calchwynedd are surrounded by Saxons, but survive because of the bones of the SAINT?' asked a huge lad who had a tendency to shout. We called him Goliath after a story from the monastery.

'Father Faustus says they live under a volatile truce.' I spread my cloak over the damp ground and sat down, the low shafts of autumn sun spearing through the trees.

'My father says the Calchwynedd are aggressive folk...' Sulio spoke between puffs as he blew gently into smouldering moss, '...and they would cut off your hand... for a morsel of bread.' Smoke filtered out until a small flame flickered alive. Sulio sat back, tucking back dark strands of hair that escaped his ponytail.

'The Saxons respect strength and cruelty,' said Maccus, the oldest among us yet also the smallest. 'So maybe that's why they leave the Calchwynedd alone.' He knelt down, cupping his hands around the growing flame as Sulio blew on it again and fed it twigs and dry leaves.

'They leave them alone because St Alban is buried there,' Vannii corrected, flicking back the smooth ash-blond hair that framed his angular chin.

'I agree with Vannii,' Bellicia said, smiling at him though he did not appear to notice. Bellicia was Maccus' younger sister but she was taller and had a confidence that made her seem older. The only feature they had in common was the bold blue of their eyes.

'The only good thing Father Faustus says of the Calchwynedd,' I said, getting up to help Sulio bring over dry wood stacked nearby, 'is that they defend the bones of the martyr with sword and blood.'

Kennan started tugging the beaded edge of Bellicia's cloak. She drew it around her, edging closer to Vannii, so he prodded her with a twig.

'Kennan, don't.' She glared at him.

'Luca,' Maccus bought the attention back to me, 'tell us then, the story of St Alban.' The small fire leaped and grew, radiating warmth as we huddled around it.

'Well, it was in the days when the towns were new, and the

Romans liked to kill any Christians they found. Alban was a poor man going about his business when he met a terrified priest chased by soldiers.'

'Did the soldiers CATCH him?' asked Goliath.

'No. Alban hid the priest in his house for several days. And he learned the teachings of Christ and converted... But then the soldiers found them.'

'And did they KILL them?'

'No. Alban helped the priest to escape but was captured himself. He was taken before the governor, a cruel man who was sacrificing a cockerel to one of his many gods...'

'Did he EAT the cockerel?'

'Goliath,' Sulio laughed, 'you're always thinking about eating.'

'With blood dripping from his blade,' I tried to keep a serious tone to my words as Faustus had done, 'he demanded Alban deny Christ. But Alban would not.'

'Did he kill him THEN?'

'Aww, Goliath,' the others groaned. Kennan and Vannii starting wrestling and Bellicia was shoved aside as they deliberately jostled into me.

Ignoring them, Maccus said, 'Come on, Luca, what happened to Alban?'

I shoved Kennan out of the way and continued. 'He was so enraged, he had Alban flogged with a many-tailed lash. In agony, skin flailed from his back, he still refused to deny Christ. So, the governor ordered him to be beheaded on the hill for all to witness.'

'They DO kill him!'

We all groaned at Goliath again.

'Not yet. He was dragged away, but so many people gathered about and the bridge over the river was unpassable. Alban, his skin in bleeding ribbons all over his back, had no wish to prolong his death any further, so he prayed for a miracle…'

'Did he pray for God to save him?' asked Sulio.

'Surprisingly, no. But the river-bed dried up! And he was taken up the hill without delay. People were overcome by the miracle and fell at his feet, including one of the soldiers. That soldier was pulled to his knees and his head was chopped off. Alban was pushed down into the man's blood…'

'NOW do they kill him?'

Vannii threw a handful of leaves over Goliath and Bellicia laughed.

'So, the miracle was the river drying up? A strange thing to pray for,' Sulio said, and I had thought it too.

'Alban praised the Lord for the beautiful flowers growing on the hilltop and all the wonderful creations…'

'Did he really?'

'And then?'

'Then they struck off his head – and at that very moment, the executioner's eyes popped out so he could not see and rejoice over the death.'

'So they DID kill him!' Goliath exclaimed. 'I KNEW it.'

Kennan and Vannii jumped on him and we all joined in laughing and rolling in the leaf litter. As we went back to the fire Kennan reached out to Bellicia again.

'Kennan!' She slapped at his hand.

'You've leaves tangled in your hair,' he said defensively. She flicked her long blonde waves away from him, peppered with leaves. We all sat once more; the bold flames had drawn the darkness in faster, giving our faces a new glow in the twilight.

'His EYES popped out!' Goliath screwed up his face as he imagined the scene.

'But what of his finger? Someone must have stolen it.'

'Yeah,' said Vannii, nodding at Sulio, 'and if it's found, the Calchwynedd will surely want it back.'

'That might bring trouble for all of us.'

'But Maccus, there'll be trouble enough if the relic is *not* found.'

'Yeah, without the relic we may NEVER be rid of the Jutes and the Saxons.'

'The person who finds the relic will be a hero,' Kennan added.

'Maybe we should search for it!' Vannii always liked to be the hero, though I admit, it had crossed my mind too.

'But such a thing would never be around here,' Sulio said. 'We stand no chance of finding it.'

'But what if…' My imagination took over my reason. 'What if, with the news of Ambrosius' death, far away in Dumnonia, a messenger was sent? A rider on a white stallion with red tassel bridle galloped over hill and vale, through meadow and forest, carrying the treasures of the king in his saddlebag to pass on to another – including the silken strip with the finger bones of the saint. What if he had ridden right here?' The gang were quiet.

'…Perhaps a thread of silk, flowing from the saddlebag, snagged on the blackthorn, pulling it silently from the bag and into the undergrowth as he rode away. What if, the fading, rotting silk has become one with the woodland – here in the ground we tread?'

The idea hung between us.

Somewhere nearby, the relic was waiting to be discovered.

4

I suppose it was inevitable that friendships would dilute our brotherly bond. Kennan shared easy mocking jokes with Vannii. I was drawn to the quiet, gentle Maccus, his self-doubt a mirror of my own. And as my learning improved, I had less need of my brother's shadow or the warmth of his shoulder against mine. While Kennan was popular and fun, I gave them stories of legends and heroes. For Kennan, play became rougher and malice crept in.

One day at the Glenring, he started a tumble. I was reluctant but he was not giving up. We wrestled as the others laughed. I ignored a painful twist in my arm but when my elbow hit his nose, he came at me wildly and Maccus stepped in.

'That's enough. Stop!'

Maccus took a fist to his eye that purpled for days. That fist was mine.

I was angry with Kennan but also ashamed, so I kept out of everyone's way. I began to make a new shaft for my hand-axe, rubbing the ashwood with sand and leather to smooth it.

'That is taking a good shape,' Mother said. Kennan was immediately at her side to see.

'That stick is mine! Luca should give it back.'

'How is that yours?' Mother asked. 'It's a stick.'

'But I found it and Luca took it.'

'You didn't want it! You threw it in the brambles.' I rubbed a raw scratch down the inside of my wrist. 'I said it had a good curve for an axe shaft. Kennan disagreed.'

'I was going to use it for something else!'

Mother shook her head in bewilderment. 'It's just a stick, Kennan. Luca has worked on it for hours now. Leave it be.' Her word was final and he went quiet.

Later that day, when Mother left the hut, Kennan picked it up, throwing and catching it, wanting me to demand it back. Minura looked at me, but I did not want to be drawn in.

'Kennan… Don't,' she pleaded. 'Kennan, stop. Mother will be back in a moment.'

Our mother had left seeds on the trestle table. The axe shaft came crashing down, scattering them onto the floor.

'Kennan, you fool!' I shouted. He scurried out of the door. I collected up as many of the precious seeds as I could. Mother came in, Kennan at her side, Lucanus following.

'Luca!' Mother stared at me on my knees in the dirt, her lips thin lines of anger. 'What have you done?' I could not speak. In my hesitation, Lucanus seized me and dragged me outside.

'But, Father—'

'I don't want to hear it.' His grip tightened and pinched.

The sting of his hazel-stick throbbed across my hands and my backside. I had learned long ago that he did not respect excuses or explanations, only the ability to take punishment without complaint, so I kept my mouth shut. Minura, watching sideways through her waves of tawny hair, cried into our mother's skirts.

My palms would not open out and allow me to work. The stiff ache in my backside caused a limping gait, every step a reminder of the unfairness. I always let Kennan get his way, but Lucanus always beat me anyway. Kennan had trampled over my fear of our father too long.

He was sent on an errand to Sulio's hut at the far west of the village. With Father's broad shoulders concentrated over his work, I left the pottery too. The houses of Framlutum cluster around the communal green used for feasting, butchering, and tree splitting. Long field strips fan out behind the roundhouses. Kennan could not resist going the long way round behind the fields. I cut straight across the green. I snapped off a skinny willow branch and waited by the hedge. He came into sight, dawdling along in a daydream. I stepped out in front of him. Startled, he jumped back. I grabbed him within a few strides. We tumbled, half onto the path and half into the briars.

'Get off... Get away from me...' he yelled. I rolled on top of him, wedging his arms under my legs, pinning him down.

'Father said, wasting seeds deserves a beating,' I said through set teeth. He was struggling, my weight preventing him getting up.

'Look, look at my hands!' The red welts were cracking open and bleeding again.

'Get off, Luca… HELP,' he shouted.

'No-one will hear you.' I was spitting with the release of long suppressed anger.

He squirmed under me but I held him down. He wrenched an arm out and twisted free, but I grabbed his leg and he went down again. I was on him. The willow branch hissed as I whacked him, again and again.

At last, my anger spent, I let him go.

He ran away behind the fields. I knew I should go straight home but I ran through the woodland. A flash of red brushed through the trees ahead: a red cape, a white horse, and a mysterious rider. The Red Horseman from my dreams. There but then gone.

I hurried home.

**

Kennan sulked but thankfully concealed his bruises. Lucanus seemed unaware of a rift between us, though Mother watched us both with a frown. Perhaps it was a new respect, to this day I cannot say, but Kennan was friendlier, as though the fight had never happened.

Lucanus went away for a few days. Without his broad shadow darkening the doorway, Minura rocked in his chair by the fire and Mother sang as she prepared cabbage soup. We hated that smell and wrinkled our noses.

'Shall we fish?' Kennan said, smiling.

With no work in the pottery, I agreed. The nearby stream widens at the beaver dam and just before is a good place to fish. I waded in knee-deep to the mid-stream current to catch minnows or lamprey. Catching little but my reflection, I noticed my skinny arms and bony shoulders. Kennan, much bigger, already had the chunky torso of Lucanus. My hair still raven black, his brown with sun-lightened wisps. I watched him hunting roach in the shadows. He kept so still, but then grabbed at the water, raising a writhing silver body out onto the bank.

It was a pike, the biggest fish we had seen. He snatched it upwards so fast it slipped from his grip, flying over the bushes and landing with a wet slap on the rocks. Twitching, it tried to return to the river, giving up as it tangled itself in the bush stems. Speckled like bark with a gasping mouth, we watched as it died.

'It's huge! See the teeth!' I was amazed.

'I wish Father was here, he'll never believe it!'

'Put it on that big rock and I'll mark around it. We will never forget it then.'

I scratched out the shape of the huge fish and we chipped at the outline to deepen it. Walking back with the fish, Kennan put his arm around my shoulders. I turned and smiled up at him.

5

Mother was ill. Father said it was *women's worries*. I asked what he meant. 'Don't ask questions, Luca,' he snapped. Kennan jumped out and spun her around, trying to make her laugh. She struck him with her empty reed basket, beating him over the head with it. He skulked off. Later, I found her in the field, staring at her turnip seedlings, overgrowing their wooden crate and waiting to be planted out. She stood still, trowel in hand, but with a sadness that caught in my throat.

'What is it, Mother?'

She did not reply. Uncertain, I guided her back to sit on a stump.

'Sit, Mother. Listen, the blackbird is singing for you.' I prised the trowel from her grip and began her work. She sat for a time, but as I finished, she stood up and placed her palm lightly against my cheek.

'Go to Veryan Hen,' she told me. 'Ask for the herbs he gave me before.' She sniffed away tears she did not want seen. Smoothing her gown, she stood tall and strode gracefully back into the house.

Veryan Hen was the healer. No-one could say how old he was. Permanently bent over, his head twisted sideways as he looked at me. His skin was weathered thin, baggy and wrinkled. His hand trembled as he held it out to mine, but his grip was strong. He made me think of the ancient yew tree, gnarled and twisted on the outside, but inside as alive as the fresh green shoots. He seemed to have been expecting the request for the herbs.

'…Lavender and yarrow…' He muttered plant names as he picked out dried leaves, seed heads, and stems, and placed them in a small pot over his fire. 'Dandelion and flax.'

Though I had known the old man all my life, this was the first time I'd been alone with him. There were rumours about him; he had sailed to faraway places, he had been in a ruthless gang, riding a war horse into east Saxons lands and returning in blood-stained victory. And he served King Aurelius for a time.

'You know everyone in these parts, don't you?' I asked, my mind on the Red Horseman I had seen weaving through trees in the woodland.

'I have lived in this place many years, but also in others. People come and go and, though I know most, I would not claim to know all… Motherwort and thyme…'

'There's a man… he appears now and then… on a white horse and wearing a red cloak. Then vanishes. The others never see him, just me… almost as if he doesn't exist.'

'Valerian… sage.'

'I've seen him on my way to the monastery, maybe watching for someone… but there's few come and go that way but me.'

'So, then…' He blew softly into the pot as it began to steam. 'That's why it's only you who sees him. Or perhaps you see what you want to see. The mind fools the eyes.'

'My father says old men talk in riddles.'

'Your father? Hmm, Lucanus. He is a skilled craftsman but… well, you are not like him at all, are you? How old are you now?'

'Eleven.' I watched him stir and grind the contents of the pot to a paste. 'Will my mother be alright?'

'She will.'

I waited for him to say something more about what ailed her, but he did not. 'She says, you were the only familiar face here when she came to the village. I think she misses her old life in Glevum.'

'Village life is certainly different from the royal court. I spent too much of my time there when I should have been here with my wife. I look back now and most of it is best forgotten. Hold this.' I took the pot as he crushed a piece of charcoal into the mixture.

'You knew my grandfather then?'

'I did.'

I waited but he gave me no more. 'Tell me about him.'

'Now, stir that for me.'

'My grandfather?'

He twisted his head to look at me again. 'Atto was a good man.'

He gave out a long sigh. 'His sudden death changed everything that summer. Aurelius—'

'*Sudden* death?' I had never considered the manner of his death. '*How* did he die?'

The old man said nothing.

'Tell me. Were you there?'

'Those were difficult days I prefer not to think of.' He grabbed my arm and pulled me to sit down, our faces now level. 'I will say only this, Aurelius has a habit of finding enemies wherever he looks. Enemies are easily made but hard to undo. It was *Atto* who kept unity among the Dobunni and the focus on Cynric's men – the real enemies. But in doing so, he overlooked an enemy closer to home, and that is what killed him in the end.'

I resisted pushing for more.

'The ability to detect the true enemy eludes most men.' He busied himself putting things away. 'I once happened on an enemy at sea, circled by sharks…'

He was lost in his memory. 'Sharks? Did he drown? Was he eaten?'

'A terrible death for any man.'

'So, did you see him die?'

'No. I pulled him from the teeth of the shark. Though he was a man I'd grown to hate, competed with all my life, and who I considered the worst person in the world.'

'So, what happened?'

The old man sat down opposite me and I heard the grinding of his knees. 'I sailed my small craft right at him. His hand grasped mine as I passed. I pulled with all my strength and his grip was not letting go. He slipped from the sea, his leg bitten ragged, but he survived. We were stuck in the small boat together nine days, learning more of each other than we had our whole lives.' I watched his face as he talked, realising the creases and blemishes stemmed from years of salt, wind, and sun. 'We became the best of friends for many years. But he is a Jute and our lives have taken different paths, even so he became like a brother I would die for.'

'A Jute? But they are our enemies!'

'Not all,' he raised a wiry eyebrow, 'despite what most folk in these parts will have you believe. I was born in Jutarnum. I grew up among the Jutes on the southern shores, some good, some bad. It is the leaders of men who should be judged. King Cynric is determined to bring trouble on the heads of all Britons, but…'

'Father Faustus says, they're barely human, they're demons sent to punish us for our sinful ways, with horns on their heads, and cloven hoofs for feet. Their king, Cynric Claw-hand, hounds the Atrebates, taking their land piece by piece. Ours will be next. Maybe, one day, *I* will fight them.'

'Father Faustus, eh? Have you met any of these folk you declare as *demons*?' His eyes gleamed. He was laughing at me.

'Should I wait 'til they come to kill me before deciding what they are? Is that what you did?'

He smiled. 'A good point and well answered, my young friend. But know this, behind every enemy is a story, the past is never a simple thing… Be careful, lad, the enemy is not always who they seem… and not all you're told is the truth.'

'But you agree, King Cynric is our enemy? When we've found the relic of St Alban we will surely win against him. My father says the men searching for the relic found nothing in Din Tagel and have crossed over the sea to Gaul.'

'I do not think it likely it will ever be found. It is a distraction.'

Veryan Hen closed his eyes. I took the herbal brew for my mother and left quietly with a certainty the old man knew more than he'd tell.

6

'Do a bird's legs bend at the ankle or knee?' Our gang discussed many things at the Glenring. 'Do hedgehogs eat worms or weeds? Do fish breathe underwater? Where do the gathering birds hide in the winter?' So many matters we could not resolve.

Bellicia came less and less, Maccus said their mother gave her more chores. Girls rarely had the freedom and fun of us boys. In the longest days of summer, we prepared to go on our first hunt. We set off hoping for a deer or a boar. Behind me I heard the delicate swish of Kennan stretching out his bow, he was the best shot amongst us. The rest of us carried spears, but Maccus also had his long-knife, and most important, his father's hunting dog, trained to follow a scent, to hold back and to retrieve when instructed.

Six of us and the hound set out. Vannii and Goliath slipped behind trying to trip each other over. Laughing, they ran into Kennan. Then they all crashed ahead through ferns and hawthorn. I widened the route, every step noticing the foliage and signs of the creatures of the forest, small tracks and nibbled stalks, cockchafer beetles and ground-nesting birds. The woodland was changing as we went deeper.

'Come on, Luca. Keep up,' Sulio called out.

'Hey! I've found something.' It was the telltale double dent of a wild pig's footprint. 'Boar tracks!'

'Hey! Over here,' Sulio called out to the others and they all ran over.

'Wait, stop. Go carefully.' I pushed them back from the mud-print.

'The dog has the scent, she'll follow it,' Maccus said. 'I'll hold her back before the kill.'

The dog led with her nose. We followed in single file behind her. The boar tracks were weaving and winding randomly, as if the creature had no purpose or place to be. The ground became wetter as we crept through the birch trees, the boar prints clearer in the muddy path under the ferns. My eye was caught by colour, scarlet elf-cup fungi rose up from the moss in the decaying wood, rare and useful, according to Veryan Hen.

After following the tracks for some time, Maccus stopped and raised his arm. A rustle in the undergrowth ahead. He indicated for us to fan out and around. We placed every foot with great care as if the world beneath might crack. Maccus crouched and held the hound. Vannii and Kennan were moving fast, eager. We edged out into a wider arc. The low shafts of sun through the trees deepened the shadows as a black snout rose up from the greenery, sniffing the air.

A familiar twang, and Kennan's arrow sunk into the leaves where the boar stood. Except that it missed.

The boar ran. We ran after it. The chase was on.

'Spread right out…' We called out to each other as we leapt over the undergrowth, dodged low branches, and darted into gaps between trees.

'Luca, go round…'

'Vannii, go further out…'

'Kennan, quick…'

'Come on, Goliath…'

'No, go back. That way…'

The boar doubled back, its black head just showing. We kept

after it, a moving circle of boys, running and leaping to keep the boar within range. At times it ran clear and we sped through the trees to keep it close. We were tiring, but so was the boar.

I ran after it. It stopped. I stopped. It turned about, heading straight for me. The ferns waved its approach. I lifted my spear, poised and ready. The kill would be mine.

An arrow flew past my elbow, then another whisked by my shoulder. Kennan. The boar stumbled. My feet firm, I regained my focus and I threw my spear. There was a guttural scream. Then my spear shaft jerked sideways as the beast darted away. Sulio's spear was next, and then the others homed in as the boar slowed and finally stopped.

We gathered around, hog sweat and fear scented the air. Spears and arrows protruded from the wiry black hairs of its heaving flank, steaming breath misted into the green ferns.

Maccus muttered the hunter's litany as his long-knife pushed through the thick skin at the neck. His eyes closed, his voice a whisper, he wrenched the blade around, slicing through the kill vein. Blood streaked his palm and splattered into the foliage. It was swiftly done though his hand shook afterwards.

Triumphant excitement exploded amongst us with whooping and cheering. Then I remembered the arrows that had brushed past my elbow and shoulder. Kennan claimed 'first blood' of course.

'Fine shooting, Kennan, but it's as well that I held my ground. A slight movement and I'd have had your arrow in my back.'

'I knew what I was doing.' He looked straight at me. 'Anyway, you didn't move and the first blood is mine, not yours.'

My teeth ground together. Arguments like this were for sour losers.

'We'll make a fire here.' Maccus, the quietest of all of us, had somehow taken the lead.

The excitement of the day calmed as we settled around the fire.

'This is the kind of place we might stumble across the silk strip of Ambrosius and the relic.' The glow of the fire lit Maccus' face as he spoke. 'What colour do you think it is?'

'Maybe PURPLE, the colour of the roman royalty.'

'Too obvious, Goliath,' Vannii said. 'Perhaps green or brown, that's why it's never been found.'

'Whatever colour it was all those years ago, it will be faded now and buried beneath the leaves.'

I smiled to myself. It had just been a story but it had given us something more. In my mind I had connected the mythical man who retraced his journey through our woods searching for the silken strip with the Red Horseman who lingered in my dreams.

'That's just Luca's invention.' Kennan broke the spell. He looked at me. 'It won't really be around here.'

'They never found ANYTHING in Gaul,' Goliath said, and the conversation moved on.

'You know, they followed the trail to a place called Auxerre, but it was a dead end.'

'It so long since the search first began, I don't think they will ever find it.'

'I heard…' Sulio yawned and tucked stray hair from his ponytail behind his ear, '…King Cynric's wolves attacked that place called Andeferas on his borderlands. Did Lucanus bring news, Luca?'

'He said, a few Atrebates living there survived and made it to Badon. Some of them children. Maybe just like us.'

'When the relic is found we can kill all the Jutes,' Vannii said.

As we sat together, the sounds of the forest came alive in the silence and new smells lingered on the breeze. With room for our own thoughts, my own had turned to Veryan Hen and the story of the man he pulled from the teeth of a shark.

'If chance gave you the opportunity, would you save your enemy, or watch him die?' I asked absently, though the concept had not left my mind.

'No-one saves their enemy, in all the legends the hero defeats him.' Vannii flicked his smooth hair back, a smug smile twitched on his lip. Kennan nodded with him.

'Maybe it depends on the enemy,' Maccus said.

'If it was a JUTE, saving them would dishonour your family,' Goliath said, poking at the fire.

'If *you* were the one saved by your enemy…' Sulio looked into the fire. I always paid attention to Sulio, never quite sure where his thinking would take him. '…would that be to *cheat* death? To cheat God?'

No-one answered. I steered it back to Veryan Hen's story. 'Say, you were in a blood feud with no end in sight, saving the enemy might stop it for good. It might change your destiny.'

'But how would you know if it made your life any better?' Sulio again halted the conversation as we all considered it.

'Might as well let him die,' Kennan said. 'An enemy is an enemy. You can't know the future but the past is still the past.'

Unable to stay awake much longer, one by one we curled up by the fire. I found a tree to settle myself in, not high but cradled by two thick branches, and slept with a draught at my back. I woke to a dull day with a bad temper.

'Anyone know where we are? Or which direction is homeward?'

Sulio, Vannii, and Goliath all sat up, each pointing a different way. They laughed but I did not. I usually had some idea, but the hunt had been a random chase, winding and turning through the trees for so long.

'The sun may yet brighten and give us our bearings,' Maccus said. It was true, but the air was cool and damp. The white glimpses of sky through the trees showed no brighter in any direction. None of us could agree. I went off alone.

'Stay within shouting distance, Luca,' Maccus said to my back.

Observing the ground, the plants and the fungi, and the signs of our clumsy pursuit of the boar, I found the wetter ground from when we were tracking the boar. That had to be right.

When I returned, the others had strung the boar onto a branch. Taking turns to carry it, no-one complained of the awkwardness or the weight, though they relentlessly challenged me about the direction.

'This is the wrong way. We came through hazel and ash trees,' Vannii grumbled.

'That was the thicker part of the forest. We must get back through the wetter ground first, where the dog-rose and honeysuckle were beginning to flower.'

'Well, you always know best, Luca.' Vannii smiled at Kennan. 'Now that you go to the monastery, maybe you'll become a monk.'

Kennan laughed. 'If we're carrying this boar in the wrong direction, then you can carry it back on your own, Luca.'

'The ground was *wetter*,' I repeated as somebody mumbled some complaint I did not catch. 'Even if this is not the same path, there's only one source of water in this woodland, and it runs this way, so we must be going in the right direction.'

'Well, you would know – something you learned from your new friend, Veryan Hen?' Vannii sniggered with Kennan. They would keep on if I showed I cared. I moved away, not trusting myself to speak.

'The ground was wetter, I remember.' I was relieved Maccus sided with me. 'When we get nearer the dog may find her way, let's just keep going.'

The boar became heavier the longer we carried it. The argument continued and became heated. Kennan, Vannii and Goliath wanted to take a different route, Maccus agreed with me, leaving Sulio stuck in the middle. We stopped for a rest.

'Let's see which way the dog will go,' he suggested.

Maccus slapped the hound on the rump. 'Home… go home.' She looked at him, and then looked about, at first going away but then coming back, hesitant to leave his side.

I moved on by myself, to see what lay ahead in the direction I believed was right. At some distance, I spotted the flash of red, the scarlet elf-cups, rare fungi I had noticed before. The dog bounded over to me and after taking a clump of the fungi for Veryan Hen, the hound and I walked on.

Trusting the dog, Kennan and the others followed.

7

Gold and gems are things so rarely seen. Always, my eyes lingered at the jewelled casket at the monastery. I had risen early before Lucanus and the low sun followed me as I stepped inside the temple. Treading carefully over the mosaic floor to avoid the bare breasts of Venus, my shadow passed the plain wooden cross on the altar. The green stones and golden edges of the box beneath gleamed and sparkled. I could not help but reach out, my fingers brushing the surface.

'*DON'T touch that!*'

I jumped in fright and Father Faustus softened. 'Come, I have found something that will give you a glimpse of the past.'

He led me into the back room, full of the scent of dusty leather from the scrolls and bindings. Crab was already there preparing new parchment. His left arm was strangely thin but he was better at the writing than me and, though we did not talk, there was a calming companionship I did not find with other friends.

'This was written by a commander in Calleva.' Father Faustus showed me a loose and fragile page from a military journal. 'You've heard of the town?'

I shook my head, the name meant nothing to me.

'Calleva was the heartbeat of the Atrebates but is now a sad ruin. Without maintenance, the roadways and drains suffered. I went there as a boy. Its grandeur was fading even then. Now it's abandoned entirely.'

As the dust of two hundred years filled my nostrils, I falteringly spelled out the neat letters. The word '*Empire*' was familiar, but it was only then I understood what it meant and what was lost. The faint writing showed a glimpse of organisation on a huge scale. I thought of Glevum, the attempted civil management of the diminished town, the crumbling stone buildings and weathered statues.

'This means,' his long finger tapped at a word – *commeatus*, 'the transport of produce, all sorts of goods came from faraway places.'

'Old Veryan Hen used to be a sea trader.'

'That old pagan will fill your head with tales of the sea and of war. He has been a drunk and a killer, and now believes himself a healer. He has never paid attention to the teachings of Christ…'

'So what does this part say?' I pointed to the next line of words, uncomfortable at his view of my neighbour.

'…This refers to the employment of engineers and craftsmen who came to make the mosaics and statues.'

'Why does no-one make these things now?'

'That world is no more, there are few of the old villas left standing, let alone occupied. There is no coin to pay for it… the men of that time and their skills are long gone. Greed and temptation brought war and destruction. It's only when we are obedient to the Lord that we can return to the golden era of the past…'

'Do you think King Aurelius will find the Relic of St. Alban?' He looked down his nose at my interruption. '…Do you believe they'll give us victory against the Jut—?'

'…Don't say that word! And not in the same breath as our glorious martyr.' The thin old monk tightened his robe as he habitually did. He ran his tongue into the gap of a recently lost tooth, looking older somehow. 'Only God can release us from the curse of the demon dogs he set upon us, but it's what is in the hearts of men which will determine whether our Lord will consider us worthy of saving. The relic may help, of course, though I do not believe it will ever be revealed while there is so much wickedness. If Aurelius will not repent of his ways and seek forgiveness for his many sins, then the sacred relic will be worthless in his hands… And he is not the *only* leader who wants this precious thing.'

'Oh… Who else wants it?'

'Cadrawd of the Calchwynedd, of course – another vile snake and a tyrant. St Alban himself was from the Calchwynedd, as you know.'

'But he has the rest of St Alban, does he not?'

'Yes, though incomplete without the blessed finger that was stolen. Cadrawd is young and has much to prove. He is certainly strong and holds out against the devils that surround him, but if the missing finger is found, he will want it… or,' he leaned in conspiratorially, 'he will not want Aurelius to have it.'

'So, if both Aurelius and Cadrawd want the relic, will they fight each other for it?'

'It would not be the first time that division among Christians brings opportunity to the heathen oppressor.'

'Opportunity?'

'Yes, of course. Cynric Claw-hand builds an alliance with the Saxons of the Gewisse and wants the Atrebates land between to be under his rule. The Atrebates have no leader, and with Aurelius and Cadrawd busy opposing each other there is little to stop him.'

'It seems to me then, the sooner the Relic of St Alban is found, the sooner the competition to find it will stop, and we can be victorious over the Jute…' I bit my lip at the word he so hated. '…The heathens.'

'I hope it is *never* found!' He looked down his nose at me again. 'If it is, trouble will come as men squabble for it.'

'Do *you* have any idea what happened to the Relic?'

'Nobody knows, and it is best left that way in my view.'

I saw the Red Horseman again on my way home. I glanced up at the knoll and there he was, just as the first time. That straight-backed warrior on his white horse, the edge of his red cloak fluttering as he stood poised and still.

As I continued, he went from my sight. Then, as I rounded the bend in the trackway, the large white stallion filled the path, a magnificent creature snorting through widened nostrils. The rider inclined his head towards me. He had a long black moustache, black hair brightened with beads and the blue-flecked feathers of a jay. His scabbard and sword reached down from his belt, driving a line between us, and the cape billowed out to one side like a sail. I bent my head.

'What do you do here, youngling?' His voice was deep and he spoke with an accent I had not heard before.

'I… I'm just on my way, sir… I've no mind for trouble.'

'You learn at the monastery, I suppose?' He elongated the word monastery with a song-like lilt. 'It is unusual. You are fortunate. Learn well, you will be useful, so you will. And might even serve a king one day.'

I was uncertain what to say. He was clearly not a local man. I feared my learning made me interesting to him, that he might want something of me because of it.

'You may speak, lad, or do you not understand my words?'

'No… I… It's just that I… I must be on my way.' I felt both afraid and foolish.

With a courteous incline of his head, he edged his mount aside and let me pass.

When I turned back to look, he had gone. I regretted my reluctance. I wanted to know who he was he and what he might want.

Later I told my mother of the encounter. 'Try to avoid him,' she said a little stiffly, the low light obscuring her expression. 'If you happen across him again, be sure to tell him nothing of yourself or anyone you know.'

'He's probably just a curious stranger.' Lucanus waved a dismissive hand. 'Move aside, Luca, or sit down, I have news of my own from Glevum.'

I was shoved out of the way. My Red Horseman forgotten.

'There's a possibility,' Lucanus rubbed his beard, 'the missing Relic of St Alban has made its way to Byzantium.'

'But that's the edge of the world!'

'It's important for Christians. Many from that place have been on a pilgrimage to our lands to touch the remains of St Alban. His martyrdom is known far and wide.'

'Could the finger have gone so far?'

'Well, it's not been found hereabouts.'

The last meeting at the Glenring that year was in late autumn. Goliath and Maccus had started a fire and the welcoming scent of alder and birch smoke drifted through the trees as I approached. Kennan raced me there, but with leaner legs and following a badger path through the undergrowth, I arrived before him.

Bellicia escaped her duties, Sulio and Vannii came soon after, each carrying a water bladder they had filled with old Veryan's rye beer, apparently without him knowing. I doubted that but said nothing. Mimicking the old man's bent over stoop and shaking hand, we drank to his health. We were all looking smart in freshly washed tunics, Kennan had tied back his long curls that had begun to cover his eyes, and Vannii wore a twist of leather around his head to keep his smooth hair in place.

It was good to have Bellicia along. Of the few girls we knew, she was the only one that shared our humour and joined in our games. Perhaps being Maccus' sister helped. She wore a new over-gown, russet red and clasped at the shoulders with beads. She slipped off her belt to show us the pattern she had woven herself. A pale pink cuckoo flower was tucked into her hair as it twisted, partly tied back, showing the rich light and dark tones. It was easy to forget she was a year younger than me. We all got along, laughing easily in each other's company with the warmth of friendship and the potent rye beer. We danced to the beat of a goatskin drum and the tune of Maccus' whistle. Kennan tried to dance with Bellicia, she tried to dance with Vannii. I watched on, amused. The merriment continued on the dusky walk back to the village. Kennan raced ahead, Goliath, Sulio and Maccus were laughing at Vannii who had put his arm around Bellicia, soaking up her adoring gaze.

We stumbled through the woodland playfully kicking through leaf litter and hiding then jumping out. Goliath began tripping us over and soon we were barging each other into trees. We veered further from the usual path, and quite suddenly Maccus disappeared. We called him and heard a faint 'help' coming from the ground.

'It's the BEAR'S CAVERN,' Goliath shouted. 'We must be OVER it.'

'Has he fallen in?' Bellicia was wide eyed. The cavern was an ancient mine haunted by the spirit of a bear.

'Over here.' Sulio found the entrance hole. We called down to Maccus though it was too dark to see him.

'I've hurt my ankle.' His new deepened voice cracked. 'I can't climb up… It's too high and I can't see.'

'I'll come down,' I said. 'We'll get you out. Goliath, lower me in.'

It was further down than I expected. Freezing air prickled my legs as I dropped. Helping Maccus to his feet, I crouched and guided him onto my shoulders. Though he was smaller than me, my muscles trembled under his weight as I stood up. Hands reached in and hauled him out. I could not see but I heard them talking above.

'It's as well it wasn't *you,* Goliath, or we'd never have got you out,' joked Kennan.

'My leg.'

'Here, put your arm around me,' Sulio said, 'Goliath, help me take him back.'

'Bell,' only Maccus called his sister Bell, 'you'd better come too or Father will be mad with me.'

That left Vannii and Kennan to help me. I groped about for hand-holds to climb, but found only thin roots which snapped at my weight. Though it was dark in the cavern, the hole was lit by the evening sky and I could see their reaching hands far above me. I heard giggles and muttering.

'We'll go back and get the hemp rope,' Kennan said.

'Stay there,' Vannii laughed. My stomach lurched as I heard their muttering. I did not trust Vannii and in his company, I did not trust Kennan either.

I waited. Dusk became night. My tunic was thin against the cold air. I wrapped my arms about my folded legs, gathered up like a wounded spider. I rubbed my skin to warm up but remained frozen. I listened to the scuffles of small night-dwellers, gnawing teeth and scratchy claws. I imagined the bear shuffling about in the network of passages. I closed and opened my eyes but it made little difference to the darkness either way. I traced the walk home in my mind, the time it would take to get a rope and then to return, wondering what innocent delays might be keeping them.

Was this Kennan's revenge for beating him with the willow stick? The screech of a night owl encouraged my doubts. I told myself it was the rye beer making me think too much. I shivered into the first light of dawn.

Finally, I heard Lucanus and others calling.

'HERE,' I yelled as loudly as I could. 'OVER HERE.'

I was hauled out by the strong arm of my father; my frozen fingers clutched at him, not wanting to let go.

'Alright, lad, we've got you now,' he said, prising me off. 'Come on, let's get you home.' He wrapped his great cloak around me and guided me forwards. It was the closest thing to affection from him I ever felt. I leaned into him and, though I wanted to be home, I also did not want that walk to end. At the twilight of my childhood, I thought I understood what a father's love felt like.

8

My mother had lost babies before their time. Three occasions I found her crooning over a bloodied rag, rocking and weeping behind the house-hut, shouting at me to leave her alone. I had not understood.

I was thirteen winters when she became large with-child. It was nine years since Minura was born so we were nervous. There was still much about *women's worries* that was a mystery to me. Aside from sleeping in the afternoons, she was well, though Lucanus was often bad-tempered.

'He's anxious about the baby,' she said.

He does little to help, I thought but did not say. One day, when Lucanus had been to the market in Glevum, he was late back. She sighed in relief when he entered the hut. Long shadows flickered from the fire as a cold draught blew around from the opened door. The cold edge matched his mood and prickled down my neck.

'You've had trouble on the way, my husband?' she asked, taking his cloak and clearing his elmwood chair by the fire.

'It's my back. The usual pain. Riding that jolting cart has inflamed it. I stopped several times, and walked much of the way with the pony.' Mother plumped up the horse-hair cushion for him, and pushed bundles of straw behind him as he sat down.

'Luca, mochyn…' he growled looking over. 'Next time you will come with me.' He groaned in pain. 'In fact, you both will.' He looked at Kennan too. I had noticed he was never easy about leaving Kennan alone in the pottery, though he never said so. As he settled himself, Mother reached out to correct the position of the straw. 'Get off, woman. Stop your fussing and bring me some food. Minura, let me put my feet on that stool.' My sister jumped up, instantly moving her stool to his feet, ensuring it was right before sitting cross-legged on the floor.

This mood was not new. I stayed quiet, merging myself into the cold shadows furthest from the fire, my hair brushing into the reedy roof that reeked of thatch-rot and smoke.

'What've you been doing while I was gone?' The question was asked as an accusation and the answer must be considered carefully, though Kennan was quick enough with his response.

'I've tilled the long field. Then I went hunting and caught a pair of weasels for the pot. Luca's been at the monastery again.'

'Minura has been such a help to me,' Mother said, stooping to stroke Min's tawny hair. 'She's washed the—'

'Good lad, Kennan,' Father said as if Mother had not spoken. 'Luca, come here. Why do you lurk in the shadows? Something to hide, mochyn?'

'No, Father, I was…'

'Just get here, never mind your excuses. Tell me straight, what you have done – other than learning at the monastery?' Mother handed him a bowl of broth as I came towards him.

'I've begun to coil the next three pots as you asked, and decorated the large jug – it's now ready for the kiln. And I've done all my chores that are expected of me, just as I always do.'

'Yes, that and no more, I suspect. But all this learning you do at the monastery does not put food on the table. King Aurelius may think it'll make you useful, but what good is it to me, *me* who provides for you?'

I had never asked to learn to read, I knew I was fortunate, yet he made me feel ashamed. I gave no answer. Nothing I said would make anything right.

'Speaking of being useful – you'll learn the way of things at the market. Luca, you've learned to make a decent pot, but making pots is no use without selling them. I cannot say how much longer I'll be able to continue the journey, and the best trade we do is in Glevum.' With much groaning and grunting he got himself comfortable.

'What news do you bring?' my mother asked, changing the subject.

'Another village on the Atrebates borderlands has been burned and ravaged. These Jutes are taking land between the Rivers Anton and Afen and care nothing for the lives of the people they steal from.'

'And all this time, we are no closer to finding the relic.' Mother sounded weary of it all. 'It must be three years since the search began and still nothing. What hope do we have that the Jutes can ever be stopped? It can only be a matter of time before they take Dobunni land too.'

I heard Veryan Hen muttering as I reached his threshold. My eyes adjusted to the low light as I stepped inside. I breathed in the familiar smell of elderflower and dust. His hunched back caught an arc of light as he poked at the fire. He twisted toward me, the grimy creases in his cheeks curving around his smile.

'Your mother is well?'

'She is, she sent me to return your dish with her thanks.' I placed a small dish on his table. 'Though Lucanus is a bad-tempered bear, do you have a potion to cure him?'

The old man laughed. 'He is worried, no doubt. Babies are a dangerous business.'

'He used to call Kennan his *miracle*. But Mother says every child is a miracle.'

Veryan Hen sat down and stared at me longer than was comfortable. 'Sit with me a while.' I sat and waited. 'Lucanus is a good deal older than your mother. He was a childless widower, given up all hope of having children.'

I never considered this, though it was obvious. Lucanus had wild silver threads running through his moth-brown hair, and his bramble beard was now lightened with grey, while my mother could still pass for a maid. She was beautiful, with her chestnut plaited hair, clear skin and dark glinting eyes.

'How old was my mother when I was born?'

'Perhaps seventeen, certainly no more.'

'And my father?'

'Must have been twice her age, I believe.'

'Then I must have been a miracle too.'

'Nature was cruel to your mother, to allow a second child to begin when she still made milk for the first. It does not happen often. It was as well she had youth and health on her side. My wife, who delivered both you and your brother, feared for her at his birth.'

'So, is that why Kennan was a *miracle*?'

'Look after your mother, help her as much as you can and tell me if she has any new pains… Well! Enough of babies. What other news?'

I told him of the village on the Atrebates borderlands and the new stream of refugees that sought shelter among the Dobunni. 'You once said the search for the relic is a distraction. I think you were right. Cynric Claw-hand's Jutes take what they want and nothing is done to stop them and Aurelius' men are too busy searching for a thing that may never be found.'

'You become wiser, young friend. Even if the relic is found we cannot be certain it is the answer to our problems.'

'Father Faustus says, Cadrawd of the Calchwynedd will want the missing finger, or he will not want Aurelius to have it. And he says, if Aurelius does not repent of his sins, then any sacred relic is worthless in his hands…'

'It's not the relic itself that is important but the belief in it that counts. If possession of it gives us confidence to win, then perhaps we will… Or perhaps…'

'Or perhaps, what?'

'Perhaps if it's relied upon too much, other measures to ensure success in battle may not be taken.'

'Like what?'

'Well, there are many reasons a battle can be won or lost; the quality of the fighters, the terrain or even the weather. The best defence is to know your enemy and be prepared. It's widely rumoured that Ambrosius' past victories were won with the relic, but it's less well remembered that he was an excellent war general who commanded the loyalty of several tribes and many men.'

'But who will unite the tribes now?'

'A good question.'

'Aurelius and Cadrawd are competing to find the relic, the Atrebates have no leader, and the far western kings do not appear to care. Cynric Claw-hand, King of the Jutes, is ruthless and cruel. He is half-devil…'

'Ha! He's not *half-devil* – cut him and he will bleed just like you or I!' His old eyes caught the light from the doorway.

'Did you fight him?' I asked.

'I fought many men. Jute, Saxon, Briton, we all bleed the same. Do not believe this nonsense you're told. Some Jutes are good folk, though King Aurelius will never admit that. Cynric's alliance with the Gewisse spreads fear into his soul, and so it should…'

'Why should it?'

'Because Aurelius provoked him – he stirred a fledgling dragon, he *drove* the Jutes into the arms of the Gewisse.'

'How? What did he do?' I did not want to think our own king was at fault. I always believed the Jutes and Saxons were beasts and devils intent on evil, Cynric had a claw for a hand, and that we were righteous in our efforts to stop him.

'Many things have been said and done. Battles are long remembered, the reasons behind them are not. The past is a closed door when people choose to forget.'

'Well, whatever the past, Cynric Claw-hand is full of hatred and is after the Atrebates land and ours too.'

'Land perhaps, but revenge also, I think.'

'Revenge?'

The old man did not answer straight away. He collapsed into his chair, stiff and breathless as he fought against the pain in his bones. 'As I have told you, behind every enemy is a story, there's always more to the matter than what you might see...'

Veryan Hen was tired, he had lived through so much. Life's complexity was knitted into his core. Every fragment of information he gave, showed how much more there was still to understand. Leaning back, he let out a deep sigh. Once again, I crept out, leaving him to sleep.

I touched Mother's swollen belly as the life within kicked and turned. She was large and her hips pained her as she moved. On a bright day in March, I took the cart to the next village to fetch the birthing woman.

We listened to the cries and groans of my mother all day and all night before our new brother, Ario, was born. I held him wrapped in lamb's wool, mewing with his open mouth seeking food like a new hatchling. There was no weight to his form, as if he were not real but then his tiny fist clasped at my thumb or my loose black hair.

Mother smiled at me, calm and beautiful. She lay in the furs while Minura tended her, and we all took on her chores. Bellicia came most days to help. I woke in the night to Mother's whispery voice singing and clucking to the baby nestled against her.

Ario cried long and often. Lucanus' temper worsened as the days went by, the lines on his forehead now permanent. Kennan was dejected. I was sorry for him when Mother snapped irritably, but my sympathy faded as his jealousy turned toward Minura. He snatched things from her with snide remarks, stepped on her stitching work or shoved her out of his way.

I was in the vegetable rows when I heard her shriek. Under the pretence of fixing a broken shovel, I walked in to find Minura in tears and Kennan looking smug. Mother was angry. Someone had left the lid off the milk pail, and a mouse had fallen in and drowned. Kennan blamed Minura. She denied it. Then Kennan had put the dead mouse down her tunic.

Bellicia was there and looked awkward. 'I'll be going,' she said to my mother. 'I'll come back in the morning.' Mother nodded to her. As Bellicia passed me in the doorway, she rolled her blue eyes and shook her head. Her hair smelled of jasmine oil.

'Kennan, take that thing outside.' Mother's voice was tired. 'And Minura, be sure to replace the lid next time.'

'I never leave the lid off, Mama, I always put it back.'

Kennan picked up the dead mouse by the tail and dangled it in her face. Not wanting to make any more fuss, she picked up her stitching, her chest swelling in jumping breaths as it contained her sobs. I knew how she felt. It was not just the cold wet mouse down her clothes, but that our mother believed she had been at fault.

Kennan walked out, twirling the mouse by the tail throwing it into the bushes.

I came out as he began winding a new string to his bow. The incident forgotten already. My fist tightened around the broken shovel handle I still held.

'You enjoy making her cry, don't you?'

'Come on, Luca.' He spoke without even looking up. 'She's so feeble, she needs to toughen up. I didn't even hurt her.'

I grabbed his arm. 'She's not feeble! She works harder than any of us with little thanks.'

'Get off.' He shrugged free of my grasp. 'She cries over nothing.'

I swung the shovel handle at him. He lurched back but the jagged end smacked across the top of his arm, tearing his flesh and searing the thin skin along his collarbone and neck. A long red bloodline streaked, shiny and deep. There was a moment of hesitation on both sides. Then he grabbed at my shirt, pulling me into him. His head butted hard onto my nose. I staggered.

My pulse pounded in my brain as hot blood rushed out. Pain seared between my ears making my eyes water and swell. I pulled off my shirt to soak up the blood but more splattered down my bare chest.

9

'Come in, my friend.' Veryan Hen came out as I reached his doorway. 'You need my help by the look of you!'

I followed him inside the dimly lit roundhouse and sat on the usual sheep hides. 'Hmm, that nose is all wrong. Lie back. Bite on this and keep still.' He gave me a thick leather strap to put in my mouth.

Gristle clicked as my nose realigned. The pain was intense; momentary but excruciating, leaving an ache stretching to the back of my head. Tears dampened my hair.

'Stay there, don't get up. I'll bring you a brew to soften the pain. A fight with your brother?'

How did he know? With blood in my throat, I said nothing. He shuffled about grinding dried leaves into a cup, silent about his task.

The warm iron of my blood slipped down my throat as I found my voice. 'Tell me a story. Tell me of Cynric Claw-hand, why he wants revenge. You said people choose to forget.'

Pouring hot water and stirring, he muttered to himself over the brew. Giving me the cup, he sat down, our heads level. His eyes were alert beneath wiry brows. The pungent steam began to clear a small path through my tingling nose as the brew took effect.

'It is hard to say where it all began. When an enmity runs long, it's harder to see the point of its start.' He hesitated and then took a deep breath. 'I will begin with a prophecy from the days of Cynric's father, *Cerdic*, a Briton of noble birth. His energy and vision made him a man to follow and both Briton and Jute were drawn to his persuasive charm… One evening, Cerdic was the honoured guest of a wealthy Jute, his closest companions sat around a hearth-fire alongside the best warriors. As a Briton, Cerdic paid little heed to Jutish witchcraft, but in respect for his host (and after a good deal of fire-wine) he agreed to have his future cast by a seer…'

'How do you know this?' I interrupted. 'Were you there?'

The old man looked at me and nodded. 'I too was drawn to Cerdic's persuasive charm. I was a young soldier and Cerdic liked to keep a number of Britons among his house-guards.'

'It's strange to me that Cerdic was a Briton ruling over the Jutes, and now they are our enemies.'

'Not all in Jutarnum are Jutes, many Britons call the land home also. Cerdic took a wife among the Jutes to increase his influence over them. Shall I continue?'

I nodded and sat back as his voice filled my head, the story dancing in my mind.

'…He agreed to have his future cast. The seer was a beautiful young maiden, stripped to the waist. She began to dance, rolling her hips and her shoulders, teasing Cerdic with a small dagger she held in both hands. He was entranced until she stabbed him in the thigh and sucked at the wound. Her chin, smeared with blood, showed black in the white light of the moon. *"In your veins runs the ancient spirit of this land,"* she spoke in a voice not her own. *"In future days, your kin will be joined to the Gewisse – whose heritage stems from Woden himself. A child will spring from the union, but not until the day of your death. Your spirit will leave your own body to become his. This child will bring all manner of people under his banner, he will be the Bretwalda – the most powerful ruler this land has ever known."'*

'But Cerdic's been dead a long while.' I jolted upright, pain surging from my nose to the back of my head. 'Is the prophecy true then? Is there a child?'

'Yes, his name is Ceawlin…'

'From a union with the Saxons? The Gewisse?'

'Yes. He is Cynric's bastard and Cynric is half-Briton, half-Jute.'

'So… his blood is a unity of the Britons – *the ancient spirit of this land*, with the Saxons – *who stem from Woden, and* the fearsome Jutes. And was he born as the prophecy said? On the day of Cerdic's death?'

'There about, I cannot say for sure. He is certainly just a few months older than you!'

I shuddered, uneasy, and lay back down, holding a rag to my nose that was bleeding again.

'Ceawlin is another story. You want to know about Cynric and his claw-hand?'

I nodded and closed my eyes. His words flowed like honey from a jar but also drained his strength and left him empty. When the story was done, I left him to sleep. It was a story I knew but told in such a new way it disturbed me. I would tell it carefully to friends at the Glenring.

**

We were too old to meet at the Glenring often, but once gathered among the mossy stones, we became children again, with the dirt of play under our fingernails and the weariness of war games in our tired minds as we lit a fire. Kennan and I showed the marks of our fight; dark purple smudges still ringed my eyes but I could breathe through my nose at least, Kennan's cut was healed to a silver-pink line beginning to scar. We said nothing about the fight, all knew he had won and I had most definitely lost.

'Come on, Luca,' Maccus insisted, 'tell us then how Cynric got his claw-hand.'

'Well… Cerdic dismissed the prophecy, more interested in his own fortune than of some imagined future child. But it mattered to the Jutes, the prophecy made him important and, with a new unquestioned authority, he ruled well. Using Jutish sea-faring ways, he generated trade links abroad and prosperity followed; fishermen, farmers and craftsmen all benefitted. So, Britons and Jutes lived in peace side by side. Many Britons became rich, but some disapproved of such a reliance on the Jutish *incomers*, and Cerdic's leadership was challenged by an ambitious nobleman named Natanleod, who called for all Jutes to be put to the sword.'

'Natanleod is said to be a great hero.' Vannii flicked back his hair and new downy growth on his lip and chin caught the firelight.

'Some of the kings of Britannia supported this rival, Maelwas of the Durotiges, Enion of the Atrebates and most especially our own king, Aurelius. The old divisions in Jutarnum resurfaced. Some Britons still supported Cerdic, but it was difficult for them, few wanted to fight their own kind. So, Cerdic's army was mainly made up of Jutes…' I took a deep breath and told it just the way Veryan Hen had told me. 'One misty-edged dawn on the marshlands, the ground became muddy with blood. It was young Cynric's first battle, and nearly his last. His arm was crushed by a war hammer; deformed and mangled he earned the name of Claw-Hand. The sky heaved with ravens as Natanleod and many Britons lay dead. Cerdic had won.'

'Cerdic is a Briton who betrayed his own kind.' Vannii threw an acorn into the fire.

I shifted, uneasy. 'Old Veryan said, Cerdic was betrayed *by* his own kind, by the kings of Britannia.'

'IMAGINE a mangled hand.' Goliath made a claw shape with his fingers and started jabbing at Kennan.

'You could argue,' Maccus picked up the sensitivity of the matter and seemed to choose his words with caution, 'that Cerdic was not a *bad* king and he did well for his people. He would have no choice but to fight once challenged.'

'Yes,' Sulio nodded and poked at the fire, 'he *had* to fight. His son is half-Jute. Natanleod would've killed all his family if he'd have won.'

'It would've been better for us if he had,' Kennan said.

'True,' I agreed, 'but at the time, no-one would know how Cynric's greed and cruelty would turn, his rule is a world apart from the wealth and peace his father brought.' I was anticipating the next question.

'Which side did Veryan Hen fight for?' Vannii asked, scorn edging his voice.

'For Cerdic,' I said quietly. It was not that I was ashamed but I feared they would not understand. 'Cerdic was his *king*, a *good* king, he said. But then after the battle with Natanleod, things changed. He told me, Cynric was always more at home among his mother's people and, with his deformed hand, he became cruel and vengeful. He turned on the Britons from the house-guards, all were killed bar two. Veryan Hen and one other were spared and sent to Aurelius to tell him of the prophecy, and that his betrayal would never be forgotten...'

'No WONDER Aurelius wants the relic so bad!' Goliath shouted.

'And was that when Veryan Hen became King Aurelius' man?' Maccus pushed more twigs into the small fire.

'Yes, he could never go back to his homeland. He's served Aurelius since.'

'But what of Cerdic?' Sulio asked.

'Needing new allies, he turned to the wealthy Saxons of the Gewisse.'

'And Cynric fathered a child...' Sulio added. '...Ceawlin, the one the prophecy says will be *Bretwalda*.'

'What does *Bretwalda* mean though?'

'It's the Saxon word for *high king of all*.'

'Veryan Hen says Ceawlin already unites the Jutes and Saxons like no-one else before. And he is only a few months older than me.'

10

Bellicia was often at our place. She and Minura gossiped and giggled together. Bellicia, being three years older, told Min what to do and Min, being younger, did whatever she said. While Min idolised her, Kennan teased her or acted the fool to make her laugh but Bellicia sometimes looked at me, rolling her eyes while Kennan continued, oblivious. Really, she was there to help Mother with Ario, who cried a lot. Mother's eyes were rimmed grey and she would lay down while Bellicia held the baby, singing and dancing slowly, trying to avoid Kennan who watched her. Lucanus criticised everything I did in the pottery, ignoring the fact that the pots I had *'spent far too long decorating'* had all been well bartered. All in all, it was a relief to visit Father Faustus in the quiet of the book room.

Crab sat trimming and shaping a quill feather with a scrubbed piece of parchment in front of him. He smiled in greeting and I looked at the fine outlines of his work, a decorated letter 'A' with weaving lines about it. We had grown used to one another, I no longer noticed his awkward arm and leg though I was sometimes frustrated that he did not speak. He learned much faster than me and was already skilled.

'I hoped you would come soon, boy.' The old monk turned to me, inky quill between finger and thumb. 'Come and see this. A Chronicle. I have been recording events of significance that might one day be useful to look back on.'

This was the first time I connected the passing of years with numbers. I quickly grasped it as it made so much sense. The year he was writing was numbered *548*, and he was listing the Atrebates villages taken by King Cynric. *Andeferas...* I remembered hearing of that place.

'This is *last* year,' he said, blowing gently on the inky lettering. 'I dread to think what destruction King Cynric will bring to bear before this year is out.'

I tried to read alongside him and my eye caught a previous number – *538 In February of this year the sun was eclipsed and darkness covered the land from early morning to just before noon.*

'Darkness?'

'You were quite small. *538 In February...* This was when your sister was born.'

'Oh.' Even as he was speaking, I was reading an entry above. It was marked *534*. 'But this,' I pointed and stumbled to read the words... 'In this year Cerdic... passed away... and his son Cynric... began to rule.'

'Very good, lad, you are much improved!'

What was not written, was that it was also the year Cynric's son, Ceawlin was born. 'Did you know of the prophecy about Cerdic and a child who...?'

'Heathen nonsense!' Father Faustus got up and paced about, rubbing the ink from his hands, muttering. I changed the subject.

'So, was that the year *I* was born? 534? But if this year is *549* and I am now fourteen...' I was counting on my fingers.

'Hmmm,' he reset his shoulders, 'you were not born 'til the very *end* of that year, you will turn fifteen mid-winter. Hmm yes, I recall that time well, I had a visit from your neighbour, Veryan Hen...'

'Veryan Hen came here?'

'Yes, lad. *Twice!* He was not always a bent-over hunchback, you know! The first time, in a great swirl of red autumn leaves to tell me that Atto's daughter was to live in Framlutum and was expecting a child who, if born a boy, I was to teach the writing. Next, he came in a swirl of snow to tell me she'd had a son and to expect you in seven years.'

'Autumn leaves?' I blinked at him. Something was nagging at the edge my mind. 'But... she told me once that... that she was only married the day before she came here.' I was still blinking. 'And I was born in the winter. I know it's much longer than *that* for a baby to grow. It must be the spring that you mean.'

He hesitated and said quietly, 'Perhaps you remember it wrong.'

'It was the day I first came *here*, to the monastery, she told me how King Aurelius allowed her to stay after Atto died, but when Lucanus requested her marriage, Aurelius seemed relieved to be rid of her. I hear her words in my mind. She said, "*It all happened so fast, one day I stood before the king, the next I was married, and the day after that I left Glevum.*" I still hear it exactly.'

He looked at me. 'I too remember *exactly*,' he said.

The implication that I was already growing inside my mother before she married Lucanus hung between us. Did that mean he was still my father? Or that, perhaps, he was *not*?

Father Faustus chewed on his lip. 'Few men would take a wife who carries another man's child.' Considering his reputation to speak his mind, it is to his credit that the old monk said no more.

'Tell me... about the darkness, this *eclipse*,' I said, staring at the inky marks on the parchment.

**

On my way home I skirted the field strips on the edge of the village and saw Old Veryan Hen hunched over his vegetable patch.

'Here, let me help you.' I pulled the leeks as he stepped aside rubbing his hands.

'My thanks to you, lad, these hands do not grip like they should.'

'Since I am here, you can settle a dispute. Can a woman carry a child for only a few months before the birth?'

He twisted to look at me. Sideways eyes seeing through my invented motives.

'Well… it may occur… that the *realisation* of a child coming is followed quite soon by the birth. But nature does not play such tricks. You understand, I think, when the bull mounts the cow we know when to expect the calf. When the stallion mounts the mare the foal will always follow at the expected time, when the boar mounts the sow—'

'Yes, yes, I *do* understand.' I turned away. I would leave him to his leeks. But I could not leave it there. 'You once told me my grandfather died suddenly. You said it was summertime.'

Again, the sideways eyes saw right to the heart of my question and I knew he would divert it somehow.

'I cannot remember the conversation, lad.'

'*I* remember it. You said, *Atto's sudden death that summer changed everything.* Was it summer?'

'Luca, my young friend, your mother is perhaps the best person to ask about your grandfather but take care, lad, his death still grieves her. Choose your moment and words with care.'

I walked away but he called me back.

'It is worth considering, these things that play on your mind are *nothing* compared to the security you live under. The love of your mother is worth more than the moon and stars, the warmth of your hearth is worth more than the sun and the earth.'

**

Finding an opportune moment to ask Mother anything was not easy. Then I found her sitting quiet with Ario finally asleep on her. Lucanus and Kennan were at the kiln, and the firing would last for hours. I stoked up the small fire.

'Mother, tell me how you met Father.'

'Not now, Luca.'

'But how did a potter from a remote village even meet a girl serving the king?'

'Luca, I'm tired. I do not want to think about those days.'

'Why not?'

She looked at me and sighed. 'It's so long ago. I used to think if I kept telling the stories it would keep something of that time alive. But now, it seems another person entirely that lived that life. I am just the potter's wife from a village no-one has heard of.'

Her words held a bitterness that caught me off-guard. I blinked away tears. 'So, tell me the stories again and keep it alive. You are still Atto's daughter.'

'Yes, you're right, my lamb.' She smiled. 'Take no notice of me. I'm just so tired.' She took in a deep breath. 'There was a time I thought I would live in comfort and status, have fine things and be part of something important. But it was not to be. When you were growing inside me,' her thumb stroked Ario's warm baby head as she spoke, her voice soft as a butterfly's wing, 'I prayed you would be a *boy*. You are more fortunate than you know, *you* can make something of your life.'

The conversation was swinging in a way I did not want to go. 'Tell me then.' I forced a brightness to my tone. 'How did you meet Lucanus?'

'Oh, alright. I was serving the royal mistress. I cracked her favourite jug and went to the market in search of another. I met Lucanus, he was kind and promised to make me one similar. There. That is where it began and no more to tell. Now leave me to rest while Ario is quiet.'

'Was that before Atto died or after?'

'Luca!' She rolled her eyes. 'Does it matter?'

'No matter,' I lied.

'After,' she conceded.

So then, she was already pregnant when she served the royal mistress. Did it show? Was it obvious to all?

'The royal mistress was kind, she kept me in her quarters out of the king's way. Though I'd been allowed to stay, Aurelius was more unpredictable than ever after Atto was gone.'

'You must have been scared.' She had told me things like this before, but it was only then I considered how uncertain life was for her.

'Yes. I feared any moment I might be cast out. I had no-one… until I met Lucanus.'

To cover my motive for asking, I said weakly, 'I suppose one day I will meet someone special… like our father did.'

'Whoever they are they'll be lucky to have you.' She smiled again, tilting her head so the line of her cheek caught the glow of the fire. 'You're growing up fast, perhaps even growing wise, more like your grandfather by the day. Now, go away and make yourself useful.'

**

I left the roundhouse and ran into the woods. My feet trudged up the stony hill and followed the churning stream, the racing water rushing under my feet, bubbling from boulder to boulder. Atto died in the summer. She met Lucanus after. Married and moved to Framlutum in the autumn. I was born in the winter. She was pregnant when they met – a young woman with no status and an uncertain future.

'*Lucanus was a childless widower,*' Veryan Hen had said before, '*who'd given up all hope of having children.*'

I passed the beaver dam and reached the large rock where I had scratched the outline of Kennan's pike three years before. I traced the line of the pike's shape with my finger.

Lucanus knew she was pregnant.

They had argued once, that heated disagreement about my going to the monastery when I was seven. Much I had not understood, but her words had been fiercely spoken and had stuck in my memory. She had argued, '*When we married you wanted a son to be the potter after you or a daughter to care for you in your old age.*'

Was that the very *reason* Lucanus married her? He gave me his name and, with no other children, might he have actually loved me?

But then, just a year later, she had Kennan: his *miracle*.

Did King Aurelius know she carried a child? '*These days it is usually fatherless boys who are sent to me,*' Father Faustus had said that first time at the monastery.

When we fished at this place, I'd been aware of our features and build. My brother so like Lucanus; me so… very different. My finger completed the full outline of the pike. The happy moment of brotherliness etched into stone should be permanent, yet it had faded.

'*Few men would take a wife who carries another man's child*,' the old monk had said. But that was exactly what Lucanus did.

He is not my father.

11

Knowledge, once discovered, cannot be put back. But it could not be spoken of either. I pushed the question of my real father aside, let it slide deep beneath, like a grub in the soil waiting for its moment. But it eroded away at my self-belief. It made me remote. Out of place. An intruder within my own family. I stayed out of everyone's way. On occasion, Kennan asked to go fishing. I made some excuse then avoided him more in case he asked me again.

Then something happened that would make it all worse. It was my fault. The flowers bloomed colour to the world and the buzzing of insects hummed, obscuring any forewarning of tragedy. Ario was asleep in his cradle, a light reed basket with curved oak rails beneath, easy to rock with your foot.

'Watch him while I go outside,' Mother asked. 'Just keep the basket moving gently and perhaps he'll sleep for a while.'

I did as she said while whittling a little wren out of lime-wood for him. I had the rough shape and worked on the grooves to show the wings and the fanned uplift of the short tailfeathers. Ario was quiet and I was absorbed. I did not notice the passing of time.

Mother returned. 'Still asleep?' she asked, surprised. 'That's...' She stood still for a moment, looking into the basket. I looked too. His lips were tiny blue lines, his skin milk-white, awkward somehow. 'Fetch your father.'

I blinked as if to see clearer. I hesitated, knowing I should run out and get Lucanus, but not being able to take my eyes from the strange stillness in the basket.

'Go, Luca!'

I ran out of the hut. Kennan was in the pottery. 'Where's Father?' I asked. 'Where is he?'

'At the pits,' Kennan replied without looking up.

I had no reason to think he might lie and went running the mile or more to the clay pits. Every turn in the track seemed like ten, the longest mile I have ever run. No sign of Father or the old hand-cart. I ran about searching and calling, fighting for air in my chest with every shout.

My feet slipped in the clay, smooth like Ario's fine wan skin, the rippled edges of the watery grey clay like his tiny still lips. Lucanus was not there. I was wasting time. I ran back. Heart pumping, my legs became lead on the return run back. Every stride I willed myself on, but I could not keep pace with my mind. I reached the hut.

My mother was crouched, rocking as she clutched the blanketed bundle. Kennan beside her, and Minura, stone still as silent tears spilled down her face. Father spun around as I entered, white with grief or anger.

'Where've you been?' he spat at me.

'Clay pits,' I puffed. 'Kennan said you were at the pits.'

'I WAS IN THE YARD!' he boomed. I was physically thrown back by his words. His intensity filled the space in the hut. The roof posts seemed to lift, and the thatch seemed to breathe with him.

I was in the yard. There was angry accusation in his tone. It was not that I had not found him to bring him to our mother, but that I had let Ario die. Somehow the two things had become the one thing. I took my punishment willingly. Guilt overlay my grief. The sensation of his tiny fingers gripping my thumb remained and the memory would not let go.

Lucanus' fine elm-stick left its traces in red lines down my back. No-one actually said I had let him die, but I saw it in every look, every blink of the eye, every turn of the head, every intake of breath. I knew it under my skin, in my fingertips and in my footsteps. It followed me like a ghost, in my shadow, in the wind and in the earth. It tasted in the milk, in the broth, and in the air.

12

The unstoppable grinding of time wheeled on, accompanied by a dull ache in my ribcage. Season by season another year stretched by, another cycle of sowing and harvesting, the turning of dark weighty soil, the threshing of corn, the slaughter and salting, the axing of firewood, the pottery, the heartache.

Finding myself fatherless cast me adrift, uprooted from the ground. I felt misled by my mother, betrayed even. But the guilt of Ario compounded it all. The scars of that beating still tingled with wretchedness. I took my place, I played my part, I did what I should with my heart disconnected. On sadder days I went up to the pike rock, to try to catch something of a better time.

My reflection in the water showed dark hair on my lip and tufts on my chin. My hair thicker, longer, but still as black as a raven. My jaw gave a squarer shape to my face. I was fifteen and becoming a man.

'Luca!'

Kennan was upstream, fishing of course.

'Luca, have you come to join me?' For a moment he looked pleased. Then he scowled. 'Oh, I see. You come here to be on your *own,* of course.' He stepped from the shallows onto the bank, shaking his head. He had grown used to tying back the long curls on the top of his head. He looked older too. 'What a surprise, you have nothing to say!'

He stared at me, challenging. But I could think of nothing I wanted to say in reply.

'You've wallowed long enough. Or is it that you think you're better than me?' He threw a stone in the water. 'You prefer the company of old Veryan Hen, or that old monk, Faustus?'

'No, it's not that…' I did not have the words to explain.

'Come on, Luca.' He shoved me hard in the shoulder. 'What is it with you?' He shoved me again. Did he think wrestling like children would make things better? 'We used to be close, then you attacked me over Minura. You ignore me. Or you argue with me. You never fish or hunt with me now.'

I *did* want to say something but no words came.

'Come *on*, Luca!' He shoved me a third time. Hard. Though he was taller and heftier than me, I grabbed his wrist and twisted it. A smile flicked at the corner of his mouth.

'Why did you *lie*?' The question came out of the bile in my throat. '*Why* say Father was at the pits when he was not?' A year had gone by with the question unasked and it threw him off balance. He stepped back uncertain.

'I don't know why! …I was just… frustrated with you. You changed, you were distant, even then. Even *before* Ario died. You were angry all the time. Now you're impossible.'

'It wasn't anger.'

'What then?'

'Do you ever just wonder… why Father *always* blames me? Why he favours *you*?'

He frowned, puzzled, as if he had never wondered at all. 'Are you trying to deflect the blame for Ario onto *me*?'

'No, that's not what I—' But I could not really tell him what I meant, could I?

'Well, *you* let him die.' Tears of resentment gleamed in his eyes. I'd seen it years before when Father thrashed him. 'It was nothing to do with *me*, Luca. It was *you*.'

'But I did not *know*... I could *not* have saved him. What could I have done? What would *you* have done?'

'Just shut up.'

Typical Kennan, when out of his depth he lashed out. He shoved me back a fourth time. 'I prefer it when you say nothing.' He spat into the reeds and walked off.

It was easier being alone.

I was lying in the long grass in the poppy meadow with the sun warming me. I watched two owls play, young ones just discovering the world beyond their nest. I was entranced, I had not seen their like before. Then at the edge of my vision, a flowing red cape passed through the birch trees beyond. I got up and as I approached the white horse dipped its head, and the Red Horseman greeted me politely.

'I've been watching two owls play together across the meadow,' I said, with no idea how to make proper conversation with this stranger.

'I've seen them too, so I have,' he replied, to my surprise. 'I've seen others like them, nearer the sea.'

I liked the song-like lilt to his voice, the way he lengthened words. I wanted him to speak some more. I watched him closely; his black hair set off the blue flecks of the jay feathers that sprung from the thin plaits that held them. His cheekbones were clearly defined with a weathered bronze tint above the long drooping moustache. I wondered how old he was. I realised I was staring so quickly said, 'They have yellow eyes. The mother is mottled brown. I've never seen them before.'

'I'm pleased to find a fellow who watches the birds.' He smiled. I smiled back. 'You can learn much about life from the birds, so you can. The yellow gleam of their eyes means they hunt in the daylight.'

'Well, I'll be watching, I'd like to see one make a catch.'

'They'll be looking for voles or field mice, I imagine. Next time I see you perhaps *you* will tell me.' He turned away but changed his mind and turned back. 'We have met a few times around here. It is good to make conversation with you. You have a quiet mind, so you do. Not like some jabbering youngsters I know. Yet I do not know your name.'

'And I do not know yours.'

He stared. Not offering his name. So I gave him mine.

'I am Luca.' I smiled, glad to have shared something of myself with him.

'Then good day to you, Luca. I hope to see you again soon.'

And he was gone. I returned home, whistling, a lightness returned to my step but still not knowing his name.

Not long after, Lucanus returned from the market in good spirits.

'What news do you bring?' my mother asked, wiping wet hands on her skirt.

'Well, this is interesting – Cadrawd of the Calchwynedd has got wind of the Relic of St Alban and led his warriors to Dunovaria...'

I froze. The place was somehow connected to Father Faustus.

'Don't stand there, Luca, you block the heat from the fire.'

'Where is Dur..no..vara?' Minura asked. She often found ways to draw the attention from me.

'South. In the old Durotriges land, now part of Dumnonia.'

'But what was he doing there, Father?' Minura asked, clearing his chair for him to sit down. He tuned to her. 'Well…' He paused as we all waited. 'First, I am hungry.'

Mother already had a platter of smoked pork and rye bread and passed it to him before he even finished speaking. He began to eat as we waited, revelling in the anticipation he was creating. Then I remembered, Dunovaria was the place Father Faustus told me he trained as a young novice; I slunk back to the cold wattle wall.

'…So… an aged monk from that place, confessed with his dying breath that the relic was placed in a golden casket.'

'Oooh, a gold casket?' Minura's eyes lit up. My heart sank.

'Aye, a casket with images of Christ on its lid and all studded with precious jewels… But then the old fellow died before he could say where it went!'

It simply could not be the casket at the monastery. Just a coincidence.

'And did Cadrawd find it?' Kennan asked.

'Apparently not. King Aurelius, not to be outdone, sent his men to search the place. The monastery has been well and truly ransacked.'

'And did Aurelius not find it either?'

'No. It remains lost, for now. But it cannot be long.'

'Other monks might know,' Kennan added.

'All the monks of that place will have been… questioned. It may be there's no-one left alive who knows anymore of the casket or the relic. But I'm thinking a gold thing like that will be easier to find than some dusty old finger bones, and surely, it'll not be long now before it is discovered. Anyway,' Lucanus unlaced his worn boots, 'enough of this. You boys will come with me again next time. There'll be the usual mid-summer festivities, always a bigger crowd and rowdier than ever. The market will be twice as busy. Besides, more people means more trouble.'

**

Pushing aside thoughts of Father Faustus and gold caskets from my mind, I was glad to be leaving the confines of the village and going to Glevum again. We had grown so big and, with the pots loaded in straw-lined baskets, there was no room on the cart for us all so we took turns to walk the nine miles. It was hot. The shimmer of heat over the baked earth appeared to breathe flies. Lucanus grumbled about his back, both when he walked and when he sat too long in the jolting cart. The nearer we got to the town, the more travellers we shared the road with. Two lads, barefoot and tattered, hoisted a rickety barrow onto the cobbles in front of us.

'The Andeferas boys,' Lucanus muttered, slowing the pony to let them get ahead. 'They're often in Glevum, looking for things to steal. Watch out for them, they're trouble.'

The taller lad was pushing the hand-cart packed with their belongings, while the other skinny fellow weaved around looking about nervously.

'Andeferas?' It was the place Father Faustus had written in his chronicle, a place the Jutes had attacked.

'Aye, they're Atrebates. When their home in Andeferas was burned, they took refuge here like many others.'

'Their home was burned?' Kennan asked.

'Aye, family murdered by Jutes when Cynric Claw-hand sent his dogs to pillage and burn is what I heard.'

'So, they've nothing but the things on that cart?' I tried to imagine their lives.

'Nothing. They just steal and beg from one market to the next, probably just trekked over the hills from Corinium.'

'But the big lad's huge,' Kennan said.

'From endlessly pushing that cart, I expect. His shoulders must be as broad as a bull, never see the other lad pushing it.'

'He's as skinny as a stick…' The figure beyond looked around as if he had heard me. '…Mean looking with it.'

'He's a hard one, that one,' Lucanus muttered, slowing a little more to let them get further ahead.

'Maybe it's from seeing your family murdered…'

'Well, whatever the reason, I've seen him break and destroy stuff and get into a fight over nothing. No respect for earning an honest living. No fear of anything it seems.'

'Has he tried to fight *you*?' Kennan asked.

'He tried, but us traders stick together in the market. Some've complained to the clerks, but they do nothing about it.'

'What can the clerks do?'

'They make the rules – *no fighting* is one of them, but they only enforce what suits them.'

The straight road cut through the grassland and the old town wall loomed ahead; a mixture of defiant stone and neglect. The high sagging rooftops peeped over, with tiles slipping and trees growing up through cracks in the mortar.

The faint hum became chaotic sounds, quickening my pulse as we passed through the gateway. Vertical lines, triangular roofs, arches and columns spread in every direction. The air smelled of stone dust and too many people as our cart rumbled over worn cobbles to the market place in the old part of town. Weathered white marble statues greeted us in the forum. To one side, rows of pedestals and plinths lined the front of the huge basilica, with a stairway leading up to enormous doors.

Peddlers and craftsman jostled for position as they set up their stalls, Lucanus got into an argument with someone trying to pinch his spot. Barging others out of the way, he led the pony on. Amongst the bustle and noise, we set up our goods, Lucanus giving his usual instructions for bartering.

'No beer if it smells like piss, it probably is. No meat if it smells like Luca's feet, it'll be off. No grain if it's swimming in weevils. No tools if they're damaged, always check first. Just take food that's edible and things that are useful… and don't let the big jug go for less than a side of beef… and if anyone should have coin, tell them to come back when I'm here.'

'Where are you going?'

'Council meeting. Those fat sneering clerks treat me like some dumb ox from the fields, they've been manipulating the rules in their favour, creaming off the lion's share, milking us lesser men while they wallow in plenty.'

Lucanus had been gone for a while. Kennan and I swung between moments of irritation and companionship. Perhaps it was the protectiveness we had for our pots, or perhaps we drew closer when surrounded by strangers. We were busy; we bartered two saw blades, a pot of wax, a basket of walnuts, four cabbages, and a wrap of smoke-dried belly pork. I had made a set of mixed-size pots with a matching pattern of weaving lines beneath the rim, inspired from a decorated parchment I had seen at the monastery. They had all sold.

I watched people come and go. A boy in a smart cloak trimmed with wolf pelt and blue embroidery wandered over. He picked up a small lidded pot I had made, lifting it gently.

'This is novus and unusual,' he said. 'The fit of the lid is perfectus.' The way he spoke surprised me, I recognised *Latin* words he mixed in with ours.

I began telling him at length how I made the lid fit, despite the shrinking of fired clay. No-one else had been interested, even Lucanus had shrugged when I showed him. Turning it, the boy considered it for some time.

'Grandfather, look at this.' He called over to a finely dressed old man with a very long white beard. Armed men on either side of him, the crowd around him parted.

Standing before me was King Aurelius.

13

'What would you do with it?' the king asked with scorn in his tone.

My mouth went dry. I remembered my mother's stories and Father Faustus' endless criticisms. I stared. His narrow mouth certainly suggested a callous nature, his thin nose a haughty bearing. 'What purpose does it have, Coinmail lad?'

Prince Coinmail, one of three grandsons and perhaps heir to the kingdom someday. He looked at his grandfather, thoughtful. 'To keep something precious inside... something so small you might lose it, like a ring or a gem. I like the way the lid fits so neatly. We should buy it.'

'You mean, *I* should buy it.'

'Please, Grandfather. I've not seen anything like it before. And it is small enough to fit in my hand.'

'Hmm, you're right. The rest of these pots are... functional enough, but this little thing does have something more...'

'The other day you said, *skilled makers of fine things are consigned to the past.* Well, shouldn't we support those we find?'

'I did say that. You have powers of persuasion. One day you will make a fine leader, if you can *fight* as well as you *talk*, that is.'

I followed their conversation and was awed by the way the young lad spoke. He was clever and confident but respectful too. King Aurelius turned to me. I blinked back at him.

'You will take a coin for it?'

'Yes, sire, gladly.'

'No, sorry,' Kennan jumped in. 'You'd best wait for our father to return.'

The king narrowed his eyes, perhaps not used to the word *no*. 'And who is your father?'

My pulse thumped in my neck. The boy looked on curiously, saying nothing.

'Lucanus of Framlutum, sire,' Kennan replied proudly.

'I know that name.' The king wrinkled his nose and smoothed his white-bearded chin. 'Lucanus... the potter... of Framlutum.' He stretched out the name as if something to play with while staring at Kennan, his head tilted to one side, like a kestrel. 'And you are the first born?'

'Sire,' I stepped forward. 'I'm the first born. I am Luca.'

'Well, Luca,' he turned to me, looking me up and down, 'you're very thin.' He lingered over the word *thin*. 'Show me your arms.' I pulled back my cloak and he reached out to squeeze the muscle of my upper arm. 'Weak,' he said. 'But you've more growing to do yet. Do you fight?'

I looked at Kennan. 'Yes, sire. All the time.' I had no idea if that was the right thing to say, but Prince Coinmail smiled.

'Hmm.' He pointed behind me. 'There's an inscription on that plinth. It's a memorial stone. Tell me what it *reads*.'

My mother always said that Aurelius would not forget. All the years of learning in the monastery had brought me to this point. I looked at the marks chiselled into the stone and wished I had paid more attention to Father Faustus.

Coinmail, looked on. He could read it, I could tell. He must have seen my doubt and gave an encouraging nod to his head.

'*Rufus Sita, a horse trooper of the... Sixth Cohort of Thracians... forty years old… served for twenty-two years.*' The numbers confused me, but I stumbled on. '*His heirs, according to his will, made… this… He lies here.*'

Prince Coinmail smiled and my shoulders relaxed.

'Well, that old fish, Father Faustus, has been obedient for once in his life. Faustus… yes, he must think I've forgotten him… Hmm, I must visit him soon… Well, take this silver coin for your pot.' Ignoring Kennan, he placed a small silver coin in my hand. The cold metal disk pressed into my palm, a new and pleasing sensation. 'Come to me when you are full grown,' his head jutted forward, stretching the wrinkles in his neck, 'but do not think you will grow fat and strong at my hearth, you must do that for yourself. *Then*, I will find a use for you… *Luca of Framlutum.*'

The old king turned away. Prince Coinmail, clutching the little pot, nodded to me before following his grandfather.

**

Lucanus was annoyed. He did not demand the coin but just grumbled and found fault with something else, then disappeared again, muttering something about market taxes.

Soon after, I spotted the Andeferas boys coming our way. Amongst the leatherwork, the dried fruit, the fur hides and the chatter of hagglers and merchants, I watched the skinny lad pinch three turnips while the big one distracted the seller. I nudged Kennan and whispered to him as the two casually wandered over.

Using the same trick, the big lad asked me questions, while the scrawny one hovered by the cart. Kennan watched him closely, not subtle at all. 'Hey, I know what you're up to. You're not taking anything from here.'

'You accusing me?' The lad looked mean; small eyes like a ferret, his mouth pinched.

'Go on, get on your way. Get lost.'

Kennan was asking for trouble. If things went badly it would be me who got a thrashing from Lucanus. The ferret lad squared up to Kennan as onlookers stared. Though obviously younger, Kennan was thick-set and heftier, not bad odds but I could not let it come to that.

'Alright, no harm done,' I said, forcing an arm between them. 'Unless you want pots, move along.' The big fellow, shoulders like a bull, moved in right behind me. Sweat trickled down my back.

'Come on, Madoc.' His voice was milder than I expected. 'Leave it. Let's go.' He pulled his ferret friend, Madoc, by the arm.

'I'll be back for you later,' sneered Madoc, his expression fierce as he jabbed a dirty finger hard into Kennan's chest.

**

That night, Kennan and I lay shoulder to shoulder under the cart, the heat of him beside me like old times. Kennan got up to pee. He was gone a while. The cold absence and hard ground made me get up. I looked about. The strange straight lines of the buildings loomed eerily in the moonlight. Amongst the snores of other stallholders, a scuffling sound came from behind the plinths. Then a cry and a groan.

I raced around and saw the skinny lad, Madoc, grappling Kennan on the ground as the big lad stood by. I threw myself onto Madoc, rolling him off Kennan.

Madoc had a knife. A small silver gleam in his hand like an extra shining finger. The big lad pulled his friend to his feet. As I grabbed Kennan to help him up, wet blood smeared on my hand from his tunic.

'It's alright,' he said, 'just a scratch.'

Side by side, we faced the Andeferas boys. It was not a fair fight.

Madoc lunged. Kennan deflected his knife and the silver blade came at me. I dodged, grabbed Madoc's arm and twisted, locking his elbow into my armpit. Up close he smelled of bad teeth and hunger.

The strong arm of the other lad wound itself around my neck, squeezing my throat. Kennan jumped onto his back, but the arm squeezed harder. I struggled to breathe. My arms thrashed with the effort of trying to find air. My legs crumpled as the four of us grappled. We all went down.

My shoulder blade scraped the stone ground. The big arm released from my neck and a sharp sting punched my back as the blade cut me. Wrenching around, I focussed on that silver gleam in the moonlight. Keeping it in sight I forced myself up, pulling Madoc's tunic. He broke free, but the big lad fell on me. Then the sting of the knife found my leg. I fought like a wild dog.

Shouting behind, Lucanus and two other men appeared. The Andeferas boys scrambled to their feet and ran away.

Battered and bloodied, we were both covered in cuts. Kennan had a slit across his shoulder that was hard to bind up. I had a stab wound under my ribs at my back, thankfully not deep and bleeding itself clean, and a shallow slit along my thigh, much easier to deal with.

Lucanus was kinder than I expected and for once praised our fighting skills. I was happy. Kennan was nodding and smiling. We had fought well; the years of wrestling had come in useful. Together, we relived the movements of the fight and the Andeferas boys running away.

Since discovering I was fatherless and the death of Ario, my shadow, flickering from the firelight against the wattle wall of our home, had become that of an imposter. Now, suddenly, the chasm that had deepened between Kennan and me was bridged. Kennan was grinning at me.

All I need do, was smile back.

My nose prickled and my eyes brimmed with tears. So, I turned away.

Though Kennan and I were bonded by our wounds, I had failed to secure it with gestures or words; a fragile thread loosely tied. As we healed the magic faded and the scales tipped at the slightest thing; fear of losing it again lurked like a worm in my gut, making me shy away from Kennan in case we fell out. Maccus understood and gave Kennan a puppy from his hunting dog's litter. Kennan named her Redak; smooth fur and big ears, she absorbed his attention. She added strength to the brittle harmony, binding the family together as she grew in size and wilfulness.

I made myself absent, helping Veryan Hen to renew his supplies. He described the plants he needed and the best places to find them and I spent a good deal of time in my search as late summer became the mellow colours of autumn. Then King Aurelius lived up to his promise and visited Father Faustus. I was curious and went to see the old monk.

'He came here to search for the relic of St Alban!' The old monk was understandably outraged. He was in such a mood I dared not interrupt. 'I cannot understand why that man is so untrusting of me.' He tightened the belt around his worn-out robe. 'He was blatant about his search, so I pointed out that the relic was sacred, and not the plaything of kings. I suggested he repent of his many sinful ways, and pray for God's forgiveness. Perhaps then God *himself* may reveal the whereabouts of the sacred relic.' He was gesticulating wildly. '...Then we may go to war against the demons with the true divinity and blessings of the Lord.'

I pictured King Aurelius. I did not imagine this went down well with him.

Father Faustus added, 'He found nothing of course, but he did take away our silver candle sticks... Oh, no matter.' He waved at the air, like swatting away an irritating fly. 'I admit I've antagonised that man enough in my life, I was not going to further our differences over *material* matters.'

He calmed down a little as we talked.

'Why did he search here?'

'Why not? He says he will search every monk, bishop and priest. He believes someone knows the whereabouts and must surely be concealing them.'

'But why would anyone conceal the relic when Cynric Claw-hand is gaining strength? My father says battle is in the air, it is only a matter of time before the... heathens... direct their aggression our way.'

'Then we must pray! Pray, I say. Come, lad, on your knees...' He pulled me with him to the chapel and pushed me to my knees before the altar stone.

Something was different but it was no time for questions, so I put my hands together, peeping sideways at the old monk. His old knees held out longer than mine and I began to fidget. Eventually, he rose and bowed at the altar stone. I noticed the wooden cross had been newly carved.

'The cross has a pattern!'

His arm about my shoulders, he led me outside. 'Crab has carved the decoration, the eternal weaving lines that represent our Lord. The boy is a marvel. His body may be flawed but his mind is sharper than most and he is a creative genius to be sure.'

I said my farewell. Walking away, I wondered if Cadrawd of the Calchwynedd would soon be following in Aurelius' wake – perhaps not so lenient of the old monk and his outspoken opinions. There might be danger for the monastery.

Then it occurred to me. Beneath the wooden cross had been the gold casket studded with jewels; now it was gone.

14

'There's no time for you to go *inking* with the monks.' Lucanus exploded at me when I returned from the monastery. 'I need you in the pottery. There's work to do to put food in our bowls. No good will come of learning the letters. You die just the same, letter learning or not.'

The winter had bought an undercurrent of insecurity in the faraway shadows of aggression from King Cynric; the taking of towns and burning of homesteads, the killing of innocents, and endless bad news. Nothing was done to stop it, no action, no battles, just a talked-about search for the relic of a long-dead saint. Lucanus was grumpy as a troll. Nothing I did pleased him. I knew I was more help than Kennan in the pottery, though if I did something good he merely rubbed his forehead, and if I did something wrong he raged at me. And he hated any time I spent at the monastery.

His attitude to my learning was typical of most in the village. Over the years I had heard many criticisms: 'Knowing the letters won't feed you.' 'Who's to do his share of the work while he shirks it?' And even, 'bad things come of learning and reading.' I ignored them all as my mother advised. As I gained knowledge of things few others understood, I increasingly realised it was not generally respected. All it did was set me apart.

Village life had continued self-sufficiently for generations, disease and poor harvest a part of everyday life. There was no longer a man alive who could remember the bountiful days of trade and prosperity that had given rise to the villas and towns full of art and riches, that legacy was trapped in the inked parchment only a few could read. The organisations and councils that remained in the town were viewed with suspicion by many, *a platform for corruption and vice*, they believed.

I felt apart from the gang too. My friends had moved on to the competitive arena of hunting, crafting weapons, and shows of physical strength. They were less impressed with my knowledge and stories – except for Bellicia.

Bellicia had always been around, but that spring, when I was sixteen, a new spark to our friendship began when Kennan upset Minura.

I returned home one day. Minura, coiled tight and teeth clenched, scuttled past me. 'I hate him,' she hissed in a teary voice. I noticed the splash of blood darkening her front.

'What is it, Min?' But she disappeared away from the hut. I came around to see freshly wet washing strewn over the ground in front of the doorway, and Kennan laughing.

'Luca, I caught a hare! Look at this!' He held up a large brown hare, partially disembowelled. At least the blood was explained. 'See my arrow, straight through its neck… A perfect shot!'

'What've you done to Minura?' I asked, ignoring his triumphant hunting, though part of me was impressed.

'Oh, she's so easily upset.' He rolled his eyes. 'I only meant to have fun with her… It *was* funny,' he said, laughing again.

'What did you do?' My anger was rising but he did not notice or care.

'She was just back with that basket of washing when I was gutting the hare. You know how she squeals at blood and innards…' He laughed again.

I lurched towards him, grabbing his tunic hard at his throat, and shoving him back against the hut.

'Luca, Luca, it was funny! I didn't hurt her.'

He was not fighting back. Still in the thrill of his hunt, there was no sign of the malice I was expecting, so I lessened my grip.

'I just showed her the little heart, to see her squeal. But then… it was slippery, I squeezed it, and blood squirted all over her and the washing. Then… it slipped right out between my fingers.' He laughed again. 'It hit her right on the chest… and landed in the washing basket!'

I could see he had just been fooling around. But Minura was upset. I hated that. Her life was not like ours; she was tied to the homestead, monotonously picking, planting, and weeding the herbs, or washing at the river. She worked hard and had never had much room for fun. Kennan was still laughing.

Bellicia appeared with Minura behind her.

'Kennan, you're cruel to your sister with your childish jokes. You should say sorry and pick up the washing.' Her blue eyes glowered in her stern expression. Unruly waves of gold hair framed her small chin, fiercely set. She stood firm with her hand on her hip, both defiant and alluring at once. She seemed older than fifteen. She had our attention. Kennan was not laughing now. He flushed red and did not speak.

I sucked in my breath. Momentarily wishing she would look at me and not him. Then it occurred to me – he had a fancy for her. He always had. He had always been trying to get her attention. 'Yeah, say sorry and be nice to Minura, and pick up the washing like *Bellicia* says,' I jibed, smiling.

He flushed redder.

'Shut up, Luca.'

'You *like* her!' I exclaimed, laughing.

He crashed full into me, knocking the wind out as we tumbled to the ground. It was a dirty fight. Bitterness drove his knee into my side, embarrassment gave momentum to his kicks at my calves, and jealous hatred edged the punch to my chin and my teeth bit my cheek. Blood was filling my mouth, then his fist impacted my ribs, locking in air. Dizzy and sick, I was losing.

'Stop. STOP it!' sobbed Minura.

Bellicia was still there, watching in alarm as the fight became vicious. 'That's *enough*!' Stop it now,' she shouted, striding towards us, reaching out to pull us apart just as Kennan's arm pulled back for a punch, elbowing her sharply across the side of her head. Minura drew her away as we continued rolling and writhing in the dirt, over the wet washing and up against the hut.

My muscles trembled with effort. My anger matching his. I grabbed at his hair, twisting us both right over, my knee on his back, his arm trapped beneath him. I thrashed his head against the doorpost.

Blood smeared his face, his forehead split. Then the hard hands of our father hauled me off, wisps of brown hair still in my grip as it had torn from Kennan's scalp. Bellicia was looking at me and not him.

We were both lashed on the backside that day. A fight before might release tensions between us, but not this one. Kennan's fury with me remained. A new scar would be left, dividing his eyebrow and running diagonally into his hairline. Bellicia had sworn at him for starting the fight, hurting her, and being so cruel to Minura. To Kennan, of course, this was my fault – as was the lashing from Lucanus.

A few days later, in the early morning mist, I saw the Red Horseman. A red smudge against the brown of the hill, I could easily have missed him. The weak sun was emerging as I walked up the hill. He turned the horse as I reached him. His black hair hung in the same threads laced with jay feathers, his red cape still billowed in the way I always pictured it in my mind.

'Good day, sir.' I did not look him in the eye, instead my gaze was drawn to the three bronze discs in the pommel of his sword, catching the strengthening sunlight.

'I'm glad to see you, boy, so I am.' His deep voice was unchanged with the strong accent I still could not place. He swung his leg and was off his horse in a moment. He unsheathed the sword. 'Here,' he said, turning it around so he held the hilt toward me. 'Have you ever held a sword? Luca, isn't it?'

'Yes, Luca. You remember. And you are—'

'Come on, lad, take my sword. Don't be shy. Have a go.'

I took the sword, gripping it tightly under its weight. I swung it clumsily, my arm stiff and my balance skewed. The man laughed.

'You have much to learn, so you do.'

I blushed. 'Will you show me?'

He picked up a stick. 'Copy my movements.' He began to step to the side, holding the stick gracefully. 'Sword skills are not found just in the arms but in every part of you. Your feet, your back and shoulders, all of you in working together to the point of the sword.'

I copied him and he still laughed. 'Swap.' He took the sword back and gave me the stick. I followed his footing, we lunged and side-stepped, turned and stepped backwards. As my movement timed with his I could not help the wide grin on my face.

'How old are you, lad, fifteen at a guess?'

'Sixteen.'

'Old enough to do what you want and to go where you choose.'

'Well, my father would have another opinion.'

'Your father? Who is your father?'

This question struck me to my core. I had pushed that matter deep beneath all else and not allowed myself to think on it. He stared at me, waiting for an answer. At that moment I recalled, many years before, telling my mother the first time I saw the red-cloaked man with jay feathers in his hair, she had stiffened and said, *Tell him nothing of yourself or anyone you know.*

I changed the subject quickly. 'I never saw the owls hunt.'

'Then that makes two of us.' He sheathed his sword. 'Now lad,' he smiled with the warmth of a friend and remounted the horse, 'practise and I look forward to the day we can spar blade to blade.' He inclined his head and clicked his tongue, urging his horse onwards.

I had held a real sword; sharp, heavy and straight. Its gleaming edge had entered my soul. It gave me confidence. And Bellicia was interested in me.

She hung around me often. The few times I went to the monastery, I met her and Minura on the way back, they wanted my stories when no-one else did. They linked my arms and leaned into me as we walked, sisterly and sweet. Then Bellicia would stop, her bright eyes serious and ask questions that showed the maturity she often concealed with Minura. Thinking of her gave me a stirring inside. Or was it a warning?

Since the fight, it was obvious that Kennan liked her so he stepped up his attention. He took Redak, his dog, to visit her knowing she loved the big-pawed lolloping hound, though Bellicia told me he rarely had anything to say. He made little gifts, a clumsily stitched bag of lavender, a tiny piglet carved from bone. Too awkward to give them to her, he left them in her willow basket or calf-skin boot. At first, she thought they were from me.

'No. Why would I do that?' I exclaimed when she asked me. She became embarrassed and defensive. It was Minura who discovered what Kennan was up to. Bellicia was touched by his efforts but then became irritated when I said, 'You should say thanks and talk to him… or give them back.'

'I don't want to talk to him *or* give them back,' she snapped.

We started meeting alone. In secret. I took her to the old formal garden of the derelict villa by the monastery, a forgotten world obscured by thick ivy and holly bushes. The once lavish shrine to Flora, the goddess of nature, was consumed and disguised by nature itself, a grey statue fallen and covered with brambles, asleep with eyes open. Pulling away ferns and brambles, I revealed an old fountain and octagonal pond lined with stone. We cleared the leaves and soil covering the surrounding edge, finding mosaic water nymphs. Bellicia loved it there, our own secret garden. Clearing the undergrowth allowed flowers to bloom in the spring warmth, and more appeared each time we visited.

Bellicia was clever. Her curiosity for life and eagerness for new ideas gave a new edge to my own learning. I told her of Father Faustus' chronical and the numbering of the years, she listened intently and quickly counted on her fingers with wonder. 'So, I was born in the year 535. That is *my* year, 535. Luca, every time I see you there is something new to think of!'

The next time I taught her the letters of her name. I scratched out a 'B' in the dry powdery earth. She copied it well and smiled. I scratched out each letter. She copied, writing her whole name in the dirt. The delight in her blue forget-me-not eyes sent a thrill of tiny needles pricking into my heart. She kissed me on the cheek, her lips soft and delicate.

We held sticks and practised moving together in sword play, like a dance. I searched for the flash of blue of her eyes as she wrestled me, the feel of her was hot and firm and real. Another time I told her the story of Cerdic and the prophecy. Embellishing every detail of the Jutish seer, the beautiful young maiden who danced and teased the Jutarnum king with a shining small dagger she held in both hands.

'Like this,' she said, shaking out her blonde plaits. Her wavy hair smelled of rose oil as she danced around me. 'Then what happened?'

'Cerdic was entranced.' I could not help the grin on my face. I pulled her to sit with me and told her the rest, whispering the words of the prophecy into her ear.

'But is this true?' She suddenly moved away.

'Yes, the child is Ceawlin, he is the son of Cynric – so has the blood of Briton and Jute and is a prince of the Saxon Gewisse. Many will follow him. Cynric already nurtures hatred…'

'Then only the *relic* can save us. Let's hope it is soon found.'

I wanted to tell her of my doubts about the relic, but the strength of her belief in it held me back. Instead, we held each other, saying nothing.

**

As the sun shone, the ground heated. As the summer growth reached its peak, the air filled with pollen and the hum of mating insects. As the days lengthened, my heart swelled in happiness. The secrecy, the attraction and the fear of losing it, all mixed up as excitement within me. Perhaps I should have sensed the warning also.

I returned early from the monastery. Reaching the threshold, I heard Kennan talking inside, showing Bellicia his new bow. Standing close behind her, his hands over hers, he guided her to pull the string taut.

'Hey,' I grunted. I poked at the fire as if I did not care, and sat down in Father's chair.

'Don't you have something to do?' Kennan showed his annoyance. 'I'm sure *old Veryan* needs some help.'

I looked at them both. Kennan still held Bellicia's arm. Her eyes said *don't go*. His said *piss off*.

'Kennan,' Bellicia squirmed away from him but he held her arm tight, 'I really must get back; my mother will be needing me.'

'I'll walk with you,' I said, as nonchalant as I could. 'I want to ask Maccus about something anyway.'

'I'll come too, then.' Kennan let her go and we all walked awkwardly to her hut.

Not long after that, we sneaked off together again. It was one of those late summer days with hot sun and great rolling thunder clouds, when the rich scent of earth rose from the ground. I checked I was not seen. Bellicia was an itch I could not help but scratch. In a grassy clearing half way up the hillside, we lay in the sun side by side.

'Luca, I've had another gift from Kennan.' She showed me a plaited leather bracelet, each strip of leather embossed in a series of dots and lines.

'You must give it back to him.' I briefly wondered how much she encouraged him.

'But I like it. Maybe I'll just keep this one. It upsets him when I give his gifts back.'

'But if you keep it, he'll think you want more. It's wrong. Give it back.'

'I never asked him to give me things…' She was sulking and turned herself away from me a little. 'Anyway, you're a fine one to talk of what's wrong. If it bothers you so much, you shouldn't even be here with me. It's *you* that is wrong.' The sun went behind a cloud.

'Well, maybe I shouldn't see you anymore then.' She liked the attention from Kennan a little too much. I snatched the bracelet from her. 'If you won't give it back, then I will.'

She playfully wrestled me for it, laughing and tickling me to make me release it. The surface of our quarrel dissolved, but I was not giving it back to her. Thunder rumbled close by. A few large drops of rain warned of a heavy shower. I got up and ran. She chased me, trying to catch my arm and reach for the bracelet, but I was too quick.

The rain fell; torrents of rain. Within moments we were soaked. Bellicia squealed with laughter as we ran for the cover of a huge lime tree. Once there she wrapped her arms around me. 'Give me my bracelet or I'll not let you go.'

Her wet hair stuck in a curl to her smiling cheek. Her rain darkened eyelashes framed her blue eyes that looked fiercely into mine. Her wet body pressed tight against me, the heat of her radiated through the cold of our clothes. Her breath warmed my chin. Her nose brushed softly against mine. My lips sought hers, cool and wet. My tongue inside her hot mouth. She pulled me onto her, against the broad trunk of the lime tree, locked together. I hammered with longing as she rubbed against me. My head was light. I had never been so wanted, so ecstatic.

We went home separately. I could not stop the smile or the feeling I might spread out wings and fly. Still soaking wet, I neared the long field of our plot.

Kennan was waiting.

15

Tense as a coiled snake before it strikes. He clutched Lucanus' thick staff, a large smoothed knob for a handle, tapering down to the other end. He swung the fat end at me, a whisper from my face.

'Kennan, Kennan, stop. Let's talk.' But his look told me there would be no talk.

Swinging again, I stepped back further. I understood he was jealous, but Bellicia did not want his attentions, she never had. She returned his gifts, was that *my* fault? She chose me. Was I not allowed to be happy?

I angrily grabbed at the staff as it swung and tried to wrench it from his grip, but my hands were wet. He lunged again, into my stomach. Winded and off-guard, I doubled up and sank down. He came in again but I side-rolled away, kicking out at his knee. My toes crunched at the impact. His leg buckled. It did not stop him. I grabbed a stone as I staggered onto my feet.

We had wrestled so often as children, there was a familiarity to our moves, but the intent to cause hurt had reached a new peak. Dodging a swipe of the smoothed end of the staff, I took a swing to his jaw, the stone in my grip giving greater impact. He stumbled backwards. His weakened knee unable to take his weight. I reached for the staff and partly fell on him.

Thunder rumbled overhead again.

We were both on our knees, gripping the staff between us. His face creased in pain and fury. With huge rounded shoulders like

Lucanus, he was pushing me back. It crossed my mind to speak, but no words came to mind that would make any difference. Blood came from his mouth, his teeth red, his expression fierce. I was over, onto my back.

Large rain drops fell.

The staff pressed across my chest crushed air from my lungs as he used his full weight to bear down. I heard a crack. It could have been the staff or my ribs. He jumped up and became a blur merging with the teeming rain. The staff swung at my head. My arms blocked it and my wrist took the impact. Intense pain streaked down into my armpit. I curled in like a woodlouse, taking the hits to my back and side.

Rain soaked me. The staff-end pummelled me: ribs, knees and shins. Once before, I had allowed him to lash out at me in the pottery, after Lucanus had thrashed him. At the time I thought I deserved it though I had done nothing wrong. Now I had. Now, he would kill me.

I was drenched wet but burning in pain. His foot was right beside me, unable to take his full weight and vulnerable. I grabbed at it, dragging it forcefully as I rolled the other way. He cried out. Off balance, he fell hard.

I threw myself onto him. Rain streamed through my hair. I pinned his arms and butted my head into his. His head shot back. With the momentum I rolled with him, over and over on the wet grass. One more and we would be down the bank into the stream.

We dropped down the slope and landed with a splash. My fingers pressing into his face, I pushed his head down in the water. His arms thrashed wildly. My arms shook with agony but I held firm. I did not intend to drown him. Just to stop him; the tip of his nose just showed above the swirling muddy water. I released him. Using the last of my energy I climbed back up the slope as he coughed and spluttered behind me. I walked away, not looking back.

**

I went to Veryan Hen. Not just for my injuries, but because I knew the old man would not judge me. He sat me by the fire and gave me a potion.

'It'll help you breathe deeply which will in turn ease your pain.'

'But it hurts to breathe.' I managed to speak, though that hurt too. His bent posture made it hard to pull off my soaking tunic, but with a final yank it came free and over my head. He squinted in the low light, prodding the reddening marks all over me.

'The bone in this arm I fear may be broken, perhaps some ribs too.'

He began cutting reed stalks the length of my elbow to wrist. Placing the reeds alongside my arm, he bound them with hemp-twine, awkward with his gnarled fingers. 'It must be kept rigid for a while. You'll be purple with bruises come the morning, a black eye for sure. It's best you stay here tonight… best for your *brother* as well.'

As always, he knew everything.

'You two are young to have such a fight over a girl. It's not my place to interfere, but you'll break your mother's heart if you continue this way.'

I did not reply. He looked at me. 'Let the girl go.' He sat back in his chair, our heads level at last. I looked him in the eye, the one without the milky blurring of age. 'There's plenty of time for that in your life.'

A mix of anger and resentment boiled. I stared at the reeds wrapping my arm hoping my tears would not spill over. I wanted to rage at him but I knew he was right.

Few things can be private in a small village. Gossiping and judging at the details of our savage fight was a distraction from the usual troubles, something new and local instead of faraway Jutes or saints' relics. Kennan's kneecap had dislodged and had been difficult to put back into place; he limped about awkwardly with a crutch. Many took his side. There was little sympathy for me with my broken arm wrapped in stalks, and my body so bruised that even talking was hard.

The magic of Bellicia changed to an acute cramp deep within me. It caused such tension at home. I avoided her, turning away when she caught my eye, waiting for me to resume our connection, which I did not. The guilt of causing the fight with Kennan re-opened the wound of Ario. Guilt seeped from every breath I took and my new confidence collapsed.

I pushed all thoughts of her away.

Kennan and I did not speak. Lucanus spoke to me curtly, no more than an old dog to be tolerated – unlike Redak, the chaotic and much adored hound. My mother looked sad whenever I was at home, so I tried not to be. Minura was my saving grace at the roundhouse.

I avoided most people, except Maccus, my only true friend, though we did not speak of Bellicia. Maccus had a gift for smoothing things without fuss. He spent time with Kennan advising him how to train Redak. This mutual friend, a natural go-between, eased the awkwardness for us both. Kennan devoted himself to teaching Redak to be a hunting hound, allowing me to keep to myself and out of range.

My wounds slowly improved; the weather, however, did not. The golden days of summer had become a moody wet autumn. Day after day it rained. Heavy shower after heavy shower, grey clouds followed black ones. How could so much water come from the sky? Every face in the village showed the struggle and anxiety of survival. The crops were ruined, the stored hay and grain had moulded. Damp wood smoked as we tried to make a fire.

The murky pool in the central green was fed from the higher ground and channelled down through a series of ditches. It always rose in winter, but already it was squelching close to one of the roundhouses.

Kennan and I were both part of a team digging a ditch and building a bank to contain the water, working as far from each other as we could get. It was hard with my arm, and his knee, but neither of us would be accused of not doing our share.

We heard a great rumble from above.

More thunder? Looking up, something huge was coming down the hill. I stared, trying to make out what it was. I blinked. A mighty wave of brown water, branches, rocks, and mud were rolling and hurtling in rapid descent.

The surging roar plunged down, ignoring the winding stream to the pool. Tumbling spray rushing, we barely had time to dodge aside when it hit, crashing straight through the first roundhouse, and partly taking the second. Swirling currents and debris tore at our legs, dragging our feet from firm ground.

The main impact passed as quickly as it arrived, leaving a steady torrent in its wake. The village was knee deep in water with swirling wreckage from the hillside and houses. I struggled to make sense of it. The dirty water curled and flowed through the ruined remains of the huts. A small splashing amongst clumps of thatch and sheep hides caught my eye: a bird washing or drowning?

No, the tiny hands of a child.

'Kennan!' He was closest. 'Over there, see the sheep hides?' It was the first time we had spoken since the fight. He stared at me. 'A child!' I pointed, wading forward, too slow against the flow of the water. He finally turned to look. I struggled past him, my legs heavy as the water tugged at them.

He followed awkwardly, forgetting our troubles. I pulled at the heavy hides and lumps of thatch. A wide roof beam pinned the little one down. There was not enough strength in my arm. 'I can't lift it, Kennan. You'll have to… and I'll pull the child free.'

'I've got it, get ready. Be quick.'

He strained and lifted. I pulled the child out. She thrashed about in my arms, silently fighting for breath. I heaved her up over my shoulder, cold and wet against me, and she brought up a stomach full of muddy water down my back.

Her shocked mother reached out, taking her into her arms. Choking and spluttering, more water came from her small nose and mouth, until at last she drew breath and cried. Her father stood speechless with thanks. He placed one hand on my shoulder and the other on Kennan's.

I looked at Kennan, hoping I suppose, for that grin he had given me in Glevum, hoping to find the lost unity we had discovered so briefly then. He looked me straight in the eye. An image flashed through my mind of when I had held his head under the water. It was not to drown him but to just stop the fight.

He clearly did not see it that way.

16

The flood was caused by the beaver dam bursting. Many went up the hill to divert the water away and rebuild it. The village all rallied and helped those worst affected by the torrent. Two homes were lost. Food stores, essentials, and valuables salvaged and left to dry out. Three drowned piglets and a wounded calf provided an immediate feast and meat to salt for another day, but did little to stave off the wreckage of our lives. With the dam re-established, the water subsided but left the ground soggy for days.

Help came from the larger village nearby, and the people brought news from other places. Cynric Claw-hand had bolstered his numbers with the Saxon Gewisse warriors, pillaging further into the Atrebates territory, and even encroaching Dobunni borderlands. The race for the relics of St Alban was re-ignited. Cadrawd burned a monastery in Ynys Witrin on the south edge of Dobunni land. The monks fled. Aurelius was livid and determined to capture any Calchwynedd men to question. He sent warnings of spies amongst rural communities like ours, with rewards for information and a place in his personal guard for anyone who would deliver him the relic.

The starving people of Framlutum latched onto the gossip. Who could blame them? Saints, spies and kings were a welcome distraction from the misery of hunger. I went to see Father Faustus.

**

He sat in the book-room peering down his nose at a loose leaf of parchment, tilting it towards the light of the window. Crab was outside with the monks, though the stone slab I stood on was warm and I guessed he had been sat there before.

Father Faustus greeted me, putting down the parchment. I think he was glad to have someone else to rant out his frustrations at, harking on about the pitiful state we had been reduced to, our leaders turning their backs on the teachings of God.

'They won't listen, they won't repent. They just want a short-cut to salvation, and think the holy relic will give them it. You'd think this level of failure would make them humble, make them fall to their knees and beg God's forgiveness. But no! They still carry on their sinful ways… They'll never find the relic, you know… Never. The obsession is driving Aurelius and Cadrawd mad. When you look back to the glory days of Rome, when people had plenty, and paid for goods in coin, and respected and worshipped the Lord God…' He shook his head. 'There will be no victory for them until…' He trailed off, muttering sadly about the burning of the monasteries.

From the window, I watched Crab try to help another monk with a hand-cart loaded with leeks and greens. Despite the wet end to the summer the harvest at the monastery had been good. Crab, awkward and lolloping, was shoved aside and sent away. He scuttled off. Then appeared, creeping silently behind Father Faustus. He squatted on the slab I had guessed he had left.

'Ynys Witrin is a long way from Calchwynedd land. What made Cadrawd go there?' I asked.

'It is a most holy place. Cadrawd is ruthless, I fear him more than Aurelius. The bones of St Alban have kept the pagans from Calchwynedd land, but Cadrawd will bring death to have the missing finger returned.' The old monk patted Crab on the head and stared absently out of the window, sighing deeply. 'But in all this, it's the Atrebates that suffer the most,' he went on. 'Oh, don't get me wrong, there's sinners among them, but God knows they're easy targets for Cynric's wolves. Worse now the Gewisse have joined in – the Atrebates are all but surrounded. I once lived among them, you know, in the days when I was persecuted. If it was not for the kindness of a family in their run-down villa farm… I merely pointed out facts that cannot be disputed: murders and corruption within our tribes, fornication and devilry… Threatened, I was, persecuted and threatened… I fear a return to those times.'

'So, you were in hiding? Where was this farm?'

'Hmm? Deep in the Atrebates heartland.' Father Faustus adjusted his robe, his outrage fading as his focus switched to the people who had sheltered him in his time of need. 'An old family, in a once grand stone villa that took me in. It was an asset for them to have the dust blown off the books of their ancestors and teach one of their own to read them.'

'Who did you teach? Was it a boy, like me?'

'Yes, Verica his name. Verica, he was much like you! Yes, it was the best way to repay my… hosts.'

I had grown fond of this old man, who so willingly and patiently imparted his skill and knowledge. I wondered how many others he had taught and how it might have changed them. The memory of the gold casket jumped into my mind but again I dismissed it.

Father Faustus would never conceal the holy relic, the threat from Cynric was too great; and there was the prophecy to consider. 'Tell me what you know of the boy, Ceawlin? Some believe he will unite the heathens against us to become the most powerful king that there has ever bee—'

'Nonsense.' He looked down his nose at me. 'Pagan hysteria. Lies cast by the devil.'

'But Ceawlin is real, he and Cynric—'

'Lies can become truth if they are repeated often and believed. There may be a boy; Cynric's lust-child spawned from his sins, I heard he raped the Gewisse chieftain's young daughter. The pagan wolves may prop the boy up as some future legend to perpetuate their myths, but it will not change the fact that it is all based on lies.'

'But does *Aurelius* believe it? Is that why he wants the relic so much?'

'Aurelius has done things in his life that would shame the devil himself. It's his crimes of the past that make the man afraid of the future. He fears one day the wolves will make the Dobunni pay for what he has done.'

Veryan Hen had hinted at something similar. I considered this on my way home. *Behind every enemy is a story.* There was much more to it all. I learned at the monastery because King Aurelius had promised it, but the more I was learning the more uneasy I was becoming about our old king.

I returned to Veryan Hen; it was good to make myself useful and I could ask him questions that I could ask no other. We talked while making a brew for an ailing villager.

'The monasteries are in danger, and now there is talk of spies. You said once before that belief in the relic may be a curse if too much reliance is put upon it. Everyone is more obsessed than ever.' I sniffed in the scent of the leaves.

'The Gewisse joining Cynric has given more weight to those who believe in the prophecy and those who fear it is self-fulfilling.'

'Father Faustus says it's nonsense. He also said, Aurelius has done things in his life that would shame the devil. Is he really so bad? Surely, he was a reasonable man when my grandfather served him?'

'Reason has no place in the court of a king. Power and wealth are all that matter. And there is nothing simple in either. I've told you before, there's always more than that which you see. Whatever you *think* you see, it's only through the scope of what you know.'

'But you know things. Things about the past that bring danger to us now. Things about this, Ceawlin.' There was humour in the old man's face, so I pushed on. 'Come on, no more riddles and deflecting my questions. Tell me.' I stirred a steaming pot over the small fire, taking in the sweet smell of honey mixing with mint and thyme leaves.

'Leave that to cool now, boy.'

I sat down. Hungry for what he might say. I felt a connection to Ceawlin. A stirring of destiny.

'You remember *Cerdic*, Cynric's father?'

'Yes, of course. Cerdic's death was foretold. He would die the day Ceawlin was born.'

'After the defeat of Natanleod, Cerdic turned to the wealthy and stable Saxons of the Gewisse and built bridges of trust with them over many years. At the invitation of the chieftain, the two great families shared a harvest feast-day to seal their alliance. Fire-wine in

115

his blood, Cynric Claw-hand trapped the chieftain's daughter alone in a twilight corner and raped her. By the winter it was clear the girl was with-child. The outraged chieftain demanded a *death* price.'

'He wanted Cynric dead? Not so good for this new *alliance*.'

'Cynric begged his father's intervention. Cerdic negotiated. So, on a cold snow hill, Cynric stood before the chieftain. His breath a fine mist, he swore a blood-oath that the child would be his heir, and slit a knife down his arm. Red blood dripping into the white snow, the chieftain acquiesced.'

'A Gewisse bastard, heir to Jutarnum!'

'Yes, a good arrangement for the Gewisse. Then, when the world was green again, a swath of red butterflies drifted and flittered on the breeze, and a baby boy was born – *Ceawlin*. But, it's said, on that same day, old Cerdic suffered pains in his heart, and as the butterflies drifted and scattered, his breath left his body as his life ebbed away.'

'…And Cynric became king. But when the time comes, will the *Jutes* really accept the *Saxon* Prince Ceawlin to rule them?'

'The prophecy is widely known among Saxon and Jute. Once the boy was born, with the blood of Jute, Saxon, and Briton, the words held even more power than before. Many will follow him. He is just a boy like you but already an enemy with more might than we have known.'

'The prophecy is not so widely known among *our* people and does not hold power over us.'

The old man looked at me a moment. 'Enough to spark trouble between the kings of Britannia. Ceawlin's birth breathed fear into them like fire. The High King, Brochfael of the Tusks, called a gathering in the far western hills of Powys to discuss what must be done.'

'Were you there?'

'It was *I* who outlined both the prophecy and its fulfilment to the kings and nobles attending that day. Don't forget, I served Cerdic as a young man. I was exiled by Cynric and sent to deliver the threat.'

'But how did you know of Ceawlin's birth?'

'My great friend and sword-brother, a Jutish man who saved my life and I his, kept me informed.'

'Your sword-brother?' Veryan Hen was so old, his life so fascinating.

'I told you once of a man I had saved from the teeth of a shark… We shared many adventures, but all that is another story for another time…'

We were both quiet a moment. I was remembering the first boar hunt with the gang. I had asked them all, *would they save their enemy or watch him die?* We had all come out with a different response but the matter remained curious. I thought of my enmity with Kennan, our fight and its consequences. It seemed petty when looked at in the light of the wars past and the enemies out in the wider world. Ceawlin was just a boy, but he would one day be heir to kingdoms of both Saxon and Jute. 'You were saying? About Brochfael of the Tusks, the High King?'

'Yes, yes boy. Many of the minor kings called for the death of this new babe, but Brochfael of the Tusks believed only disaster could come from such an act, it would begin a new war. Aurelius of the Dobunni, already fearful of Cynric and his Jutes, shouted he would do it himself if he had to.'

'Could he really kill a child, a baby?'

'Brochfael believed so. When the gathering was over, he sent a spy to watch over him.'

'Did Atto not try to stop Aurelius?'

'He advised against it. I heard the argument up the stone corridor of Aurelius' quarters. Few men would get away with a confrontation like that. Atto was the only one who dared try. As Brochfael expected, Aurelius hatched a plot to murder the child. The spy discovered it, but too late to prevent a small band of Dobunni men leaving for the royal Gewisse encampment. They wore the colours of Cynric's hearth-men, hoping to spark divisions and break the alliance between the Saxons and Jutes, and crept in to smother the babe. His mother fought like a wild cat, raising the alarm and saving her baby. The Gewisse warriors cut the Dobunni men to pieces, confessing their identity as they died, their insides opened for the crows to feast on. Now, Cynric Claw-hand feeds his son a hatred for the Dobunni, and fearing him more than the devil, Aurelius' hair fell out and his beard turned white overnight.'

The old man's voice had grown tired, his old eyes closed and I knew it was time to leave him. I pulled his felted blanket over him and crept away quietly. Despite the disturbing story, the Jutes and Saxons were more human to me, with hopes and fears, anger and vengeance – things I understood.

Perhaps a new generation of leaders, without the guilt and baggage of the past, and the right preparations for war, might defeat them yet - perhaps Prince Coinmail, the boy who bought my pot for a silver coin.

Walking home, my thoughts drifted to Ceawlin, born the same year as me. He had never known Cerdic, just as I had never known Atto, but the legacy of our grandfathers stands large in our lives and propels us both towards an unknown future. Ceawlin's mother was raped and his maternal grandfather demanded the death of his father.

Again, I wondered about my own beginning. Was *my* father dead? Was she raped? Why was my mother pregnant and alone in Aurelius' court?

'You don't give away our food,' Lucanus fumed at my mother.
'Would you take it from the mouths of your own children to feed
that bent twig of a man?'

The winter that followed the flood was the hardest I've known.
Vegetables ruined in the ground. The rotting parsnips and leeks
were barely edible even for the pigs. Winter crops were replanted,
and though young seedlings were beginning to emerge, nothing
would be ready for some time. My stomach ached so hard I could
barely stand straight. We hunted often. Kennan, still limping, went
off with his bow and his hound.

Rationing the little we had, tempers frayed and arguments simmered. My mother gave some of our portion to old Veryan Hen who was thinner and frailer than ever.

'But husband, he's no family to care for him. He barely copes alone now, who else will help him if we do not?'

'He's not our problem.'

'He will be if one of us becomes sick.' My mother was right, but I knew it was more than just the weight and tactic of survival. It was the instinctive softness and love that shaped her.

Then Kennan was given the larger portion over me.

'He's bigger and needs more than Luca,' Lucanus justified. 'And anyway, he does more for our benefit, too. Luca may learn, may be clever with words, he may make little pots for a silver coin, but he does not bring in a fine hare from a hunt.'

I wanted to argue that it was *my* pots that were always bartered first at the market, and his own would have dried out and cracked without *me* tending them all in the pottery.

But none of that mattered. I was another man's child. I was not his.

**

The village needed food. I knew the monks might have something to spare, I would show Lucanus. I took the cart in the cold crisp of morning, the low sun yellowing the tree tops under a wide pale sky. All the undeserved wrath, and every suppressed justification for my innocence, clamoured inside me and steamed on my breath.

I always strived for his good opinion, but it was never enough. When my learning was useful to him, he belittled my efforts at ploughing or something else. When I out-reasoned Kennan, he still sided with him. When he beat me, I endured silently as he demanded, but he beat me anyway. He expected a blind acceptance of his inconsistent authority. I was a dutiful son and was treated like a dog in return. He was not my father. I would never use that term for him again.

I tried to leave my anger at the monastery gateway. I rang on the bell as the rooks cawed overhead. I waited an unusually long time before the peep hatch in the great door opened.

'Oh, it's you.' Father Faustus himself was at the gate. 'Come in quickly, and slide the bar across. We've unwelcome visitors about. Did you see any armed men on your way?'

'No, Father, who do you mean?'

Crab sidled up to me, took the pony and led the cart inside as I closed and barred the doors.

'Calchwynedd men have been here. They searched the place... found nothing of course! I fear they will come back.' The thin old monk tightened his belt and looked at the empty cart. 'You want supplies for the village? Things are that bad?'

'If you can spare something... I've come at a bad time...'

'No matter. They've gone now it seems – and there is never a good time to starve.'

He called another monk for assistance and turned back to me, his hand firm on my shoulder. 'We'll spare what we can for those in need.'

We stood in the old temple doorway out of the breeze, watching the monks load crates of root vegetables, salted fish, and sacks of coarse flour onto the cart. They were generous.

Cadrawd's men had searched without violence, for now. Crab stood with us, saying nothing of course. I had always though he was fortunate to live in the safety of the monastery, but now it was a dangerous place.

Though right then, it was a place I preferred to be.

'By that scowl on your face, you look like you have troubles of your own – and not just hunger. What else is on your mind, lad?'

I shrugged. 'Lucanus hates me.' I had not intended to say this.

Both Faustus and Crab looked at me. My troubles were ridiculous compared to theirs. But despite his own worries the old monk considered my situation and I should have been grateful for that.

'Yes. He's not a man I know well, but I believe he loves your mother and intended to be a good father to you…' He paused, perhaps an attempt to be tactful. '…But once his own children came along… well, you're just a cuckoo in the nest.'

'A cuckoo?' I felt wounded. The hurt I had absorbed for so long rose within me as anger.

'Yes, a cuckoo. A cuckoo will lay eggs in other birds' nests, so they will feed and raise the chick. Lucanus feeds and raises you, though you're not his own.'

So, he knew. He had always known. I did not answer.

'And I imagine he's never been happy about you spending time here, but has allowed it out of regard for your mother… He trains you in the pottery though more than likely you'll leave and serve the king. Yes, I expect he considers you a burden at times, especially when there's little to eat.'

I wished I had not spoken.

He meant well but his bluntness hurt me. Veryan Hen might have told me a story about cuckoos, or perhaps helped me understand things from Lucanus' point of view. Father Faustus just made me angry inside. A *cuckoo*, in the *wrong* nest, a *burden*. And I would probably never know who my real father was.

It is childish to me now and I am ashamed, but I became suddenly reckless, spiteful even. Perhaps it was the aching hunger. Whatever the reason, I let my spite out. Standing in the temple before the bare altar stone, I pictured the gold casket that used to be there.

'You used to have a jewelled gold casket on the altar, where is it now?' I looked at him directly. He wrinkled his nose before answering, aware of my change in tone.

'I'm surprised you remember! It's been gone for some time... A good thing as it happens – it may well be confused with... another.'

'Where did it go? Who has it now?'

'Well, boy, not that it's any of your business, but a thing like that will bring conflict once it is known about.' I had rattled him. 'Few treasures remain from the past, much has been given to the Saxons in tribute; the peace I have seen in my lifetime was paid for in gold and precious metals. That casket is rare and there are many who would claim ownership and fight for it.'

'Like they do for the relic of St Alban?' I could not help myself but persist.

'This casket has only value to man, I don't suppose God cares for it at all.'

'So, *is* it the casket King Aurelius seeks?'

'Hmph. It's worthless to him and best forgotten.' His old face looked pale. He tightened his belt once again, turning his back on me. He was looking outside at the cart. 'Our harvest was good and the winter is upon us. We are sparing much food for the village. I hope you and the... people are grateful...' The sharp pinch in his voice softened as his words tailed off.

My cheeks burned red. He looked at me with those wily intelligent eyes, and spoke kindly, reasonably. 'I know I can *rely* on you, not to ever speak of the things that do not concern you.'

'Yes, Father.' I looked at my feet, unable to meet his gaze. It was as close to an admission as I was likely to get, but I had hurt him to get it. I was certain he had the casket – the relic, but also that I would do nothing about it. I could never hurt him again.

**

When the cart trundled in, I was greeted like a hero, the people of

Framlutum were indeed grateful. Though the supplies had seemed plentiful when the monks loaded the cart, they were little enough once shared out. Lucanus said nothing at first, but when I took a bag of oats and two smoked pork ribs, he questioned my motive.

'For Veryan Hen.' I answered boldly, challenging him, but with others about, he just shrugged. I did not care anymore. Nothing he could say or do would affect me again.

On my way to the old man's hut, Bellicia stepped out in front of me. I was so used to pushing away my feelings for her, I was surprised when emotion swelled right up in my throat.

'Are you never going to speak to me again?' She stepped closer, smelling of jasmine and fresh straw. 'I know you've been busy, we all have. But you're avoiding me. Luca...' She looked at her feet. 'I think about that... kiss at the lime tree all the time.'

'Bellicia, don't...'

'Kennan is so busy with Redak now, he has forgotten me entirely. He's no regard for me anymore. I've not had a gift from him since—'

'Bellicia, I must take this food to Veryan Hen.'

'What's the rush? The old man's not going anywhere. I thought... I understand it's... damaged things with your brother, but maybe now, you might at least... talk to me again.'

'I don't want to talk now.' Though truly, I did want to talk, to get back some of the simple pleasure of laughing and holding her hand, but instead, standing before her, I was tearful and tired. I had relived that kiss so many times, longing to repeat it but fearing it also. Kennan might be distracted but I was not fooled. Any sign I was still seeing Bellicia would only bring further turmoil.

'The other lads say Kennan taught you a lesson, and that you'll not bother with me again after the beating he gave you. I thought, maybe, they're wrong. Maybe you're just letting the dust settle. I thought I'd give you time to get over it.'

'I am over it.' My words came out as a harsh statement of fact. *You'll break your mother's heart,* Veryan Hen had said. There were more people hurt than just us two. We could not go back.

'Are you afraid of your brother then?'

She knew I was not. I think she just wanted a reaction, something, anything, from me.

'Just leave me alone.'

She stepped back with a fault in her footing. Looking me up and down as if gauging my intent. I had to drive out her hope or else I might cave in.

'You're not worth the trouble.' I spat out the words, concealing the tremor my voice might contain. 'Don't you have things to do?'

Tears filled her eyes. I wanted to hold her and say I didn't mean it. She ran away. Was I right?

I went to Veryan Hen, a heaviness in my limbs and a slump in my spine.

**

The old man had taken advantage of the sun and, though it was still cold, laid out his few possessions still damp from the flood to finally dry. I arrived as he was beginning to carry them awkwardly back into the hut. It was easier to help him than to speak right then.

I picked up a strange wooden frame laced with strings, a harp. Such an unusual thing to hold. Something altered inside me as I plucked at the loose strings.

'I didn't know you made music. You play this?'

'I did, before my fingers stiffened and cramped. It's suffered from lack of use, and now the water has damaged it.'

'I can fix it for you.' Kennan had his dog, and I needed something too.

'Yes, fix it. I've no use for it now, fix it for yourself.'

'This oak strut is cracked. I can make a new piece.' A small part of my old self returned. 'But these pegs… I'll make new ones in fired clay…'

'Yes, that may work. Do that, and I'll show you what I can… though my old hands are too painful to play it for long.'

Taking his last things back inside, I sat down. He hung his little pot on the fire-dog and warmed his hands. 'So, you've been to the monastery then? They've had visitors, I believe. What do you know?'

There was much I knew, but what should I confide? 'Cadrawd's men came to search. They found nothing, but remained watching for a while.'

'I saw them. New rumours of spies are going about.' He sat down heavily, our heads level.

'You've got stiff, old friend. Your back hurts?'

'Always, but worse in a cold draught. This breeze may dry out my things, but it brings the cold right into my bones. Oh, don't mind me, at my age every day is a blessing. You know Aurelius will be here as soon as he gets word that Cadrawd has been. There could be trouble ahead for the monastery… Don't get yourself involved.'

When I got up to leave, taking the harp, he said, 'It'll take your mind off the girl. You did the right thing.' How did he know? He always seemed to know.

'I should've been kinder,' I whispered to myself on a sigh. But then he whispered back.

'No, she'd not let you go if you'd been kind.'

As winter deepened, an east wind brought a freeze. The village pool iced over. The new root crops froze in the ground. Another baby died and an old woman too. The earth was too hard to bury them. We lived mostly by scavenging and the food we gathered from the land around us.

Lucanus was a bear, lumbering and grumbling so I stayed away from him whenever I could. I wondered if he even noticed less was done in the pottery. Kennan had been training Redak to hunt and retrieve; other than chewing Lucanus' boots and his chair legs, she had brought a life and humour to our home that was much needed.

'In the last few days,' Lucanus announced loudly, 'Kennan has brought home plump winter duck, goosander, and wigeon, all from the wetlands near the great river.' He mentioned nothing of the small creatures I had caught in my traps.

Kennan and I played out a show of harmony for our mother. I noticed a new delicacy had touched her. Her complexion, still youthful, had turned the paler shade of dried clay. Her eyes, still bright, were now rimmed with shadows.

It was Minura who took on the weight of the family when she could no longer carry it. She was just thirteen, and managing her tasks like an adult. Little Min, wisps of wavy brown hair like Lucanus, but her demeanour so like our mother. Still small and skinny as a sapling, she looked so tired, so weak, but so determined.

Our breath steamed, our damp clothes too when we emerged from the warm bed-straw. I stuffed clumps of sheep wool into my boots, rubbing the seams with goose fat to keep my feet drier. Mother did not get up at all one day.

'Go fetch Veryan Hen,' Lucanus muttered gruffly as he stoked up the fire.

'That bent twig of a man may be too weak to come.' I did not try to keep the contempt from my voice. 'He's not faired too well this winter.'

Lucanus growled and stepped right up to me. He loomed in the doorway as big and as broad as ever. I did not flinch. My eyes met his. His power over me had tarnished, his edge dulled.

'Husband?' My mother's weak voice strained out from behind him, still with the will to defuse.

'Just GO, Luca.' In his great bull hide cloak, he turned and lurched towards her.

18

Stopping dead as if turned to stone, I listened to a conversation I should not have heard.

The secret garden Bellicia and I cleared and spent such memorable times was good winter hunting ground for stoats and voles with no-one to disturb them. I was checking my snares to see what catch I had made. As I approached the holly bushes, I heard the unmistakable giggling of Bellicia.

'This place gives me the creeps. How on earth did you find it?' The unmistakable voice of Vannii.

'Oh, I just came across it,' she lied. I was thankful for that. At least she could keep something secret. 'Don't you like it, I think it's… mystical.'

'Mystical? It's just abandoned rubbish grown over in weeds.'

'Well, it was nicer in the summer.'

'Are you sulking? What's the matter? Yesterday you seemed pleased to be with me.' Their voices were close together and although I could not see, I imagined he was stroking her hair as I had.

'Well, now that we are here, I'm not so sure, Vannii. You know, we really shouldn't be. You know what trouble it caused between Kennan and Luca.'

'Kennan and Luca will fight over anything. Luca's so arrogant he deserved a good beating.'

'Don't say that, I don't think you've ever liked him. You always sided with Kennan… Everyone talks as if Kennan won, but I heard that he'll never walk properly again with that knee.'

'But Luca was black and blue, a broken arm, and probably much more besides.'

'Well, whatever... but, I felt terrible about it. And when I saw him, all bruised and swollen... he looked like he'd fallen down a mountain.'

'It's only because Kennan respects his mother that he didn't kill him.'

'He wouldn't do that!'

'Well, that's what he said. Luca's as scrawny as a winter fox, but dark, with eyes like a crow. I don't know what you see in him. He's no match for any of us.'

'You're not going to fight him, are you? I don't want that, promise me you won't.'

'Give me a kiss and I'll promise. Come on, that's why we're here isn't it?' Come on, Bell...'

'Vannii, stop. Wait a minute. I just don't want to be the cause of any more trouble. You sure Kennan won't be angry?'

'Of course, he's my friend. He says he's not bothered about you anymore.'

'Oh... but... but he would've *killed* Luca over it?'

'He'll kill Luca one of these days over something, he has sworn it. Come on, Bell, give me a kiss.'

If I hadn't been frozen in horror, I might've been sick.

Vannii! I remembered those days at the Glenring when Bellicia used to come, she always liked him – all the girls did. He was tall, with smooth blond hair and a delicate chin. We laughed about it, the silly giggling girls. Did she *really* like him?

The utter betrayal of bringing him to our secret place, encouraging him, and the prospect of her giving anything of herself to him, wounded me deeply. Had I hurt her so much?

I knew what Vannii was like. He always wanted to be the best, to be right, and I had often challenged him. Sometimes he used Kennan's friendship to spite me, he had certainly intensified the differences with my brother. Had he exaggerated Kennan's words? It was typical of him to belittle me, drive out any good opinion Bellicia might have for me. He would say anything to impress her and get a kiss from her.

That cut me.

I edged my way back to the village, my heart shattering, piece by piece.

**

Kennan spent longer away from the village. At first, I thought it was the delicacy of our mother that he avoided, he never coped well with her illness. But perhaps it was Vannii and Bellicia he was avoiding. It was hard to believe he was not bothered about her after the beating he had given me. More likely, he would deny it to Vannii, who knew as well as I, that Bellicia did not return the feeling… and Vannii also knew that Kennan would never fight *him* as he did me.

There were times I wanted to kill Kennan, private moments of anger I never discussed with anyone else. But I could well imagine Kennan bragging that he would kill me.

He has sworn it. Those words fired something inside that fundamentally changed me.

I forced my softer damaged layers deep inside. My hard outer shell must become thicker. Through the many spikes of hurt – Vannii, Bellicia… I suppose I focussed on the easiest – my brother had sworn to kill me.

**

I watched Bellicia and Vannii. She clung to him as they talked in a gateway. 'She looks happy,' I said bitterly to Minura, walking beside me.

'You should hear them argue,' Minura said, shrugging.

Bellicia caught my eye, and turned away smiling at Vannii. I had a bad taste in my mouth.

I saw little of Kennan. The troubles between us were much deeper rooted than the conflict over Bellicia. That fight had merely sealed the enmity that had been brewing all our lives. We had nothing to say; there were no words that could penetrate the gulf that divided us. The fragile stands of harmony that we occasionally encountered had been broken by the next wave of hatred.

I mended the harp. I smoothed the creamy new oak strut with sand and leather. I shaped the tiny clay pegs to attach the harp strings and placed them in the kiln while Lucanus grumbled about it. I stretched and rubbed some fine threads of gut for the harp. Tensioned to breaking, they made clear ringing sounds that echoed my soul.

Though I'd turned seventeen I seemed to have shrunk. Redak grew. She ate better than me. The pitiful share I'd grown used to over in the chilly winter days would leave a squirrel hungry.

Scrawny, Vannii had said. Well, that much was true. My skin thinned over my ribs, showing every bone and muscle. Someone else who said so was the Red Horseman.

I met him on the path. Still a huge figure, armed with that great sword, his red cape flapping lazily in the breeze. Threads of black hair were still decorated with beads and jay feathers, but his long moustache was greyer.

'Well, the winter has not been kind to you, lad. You're thinner than a grass snake, so you are.' He leaned down to see me closer. 'Come nearer.'

I remained where I was. The confidence he had given me when teaching me swordplay had gone. He had never told me his name. Who was this mysterious man that I was so drawn to, with talk of spies, I wondered what his purpose might be.

'I have something you may be glad of. Step up, Luca...'

My curiosity edged my feet right up to the white horse, snickering gently and flicking his head as I approached. I reached out and touched his smooth neck. The man turned to pull a bulging hemp sack from his saddle-pack, the jay feathers in his hair swinging as he did. He held it out to me.

'Nuts,' he said. 'Supposed to be a gift to another, but you look like you need them more, so you do.'

Nuts? I looked into the sack, full of smooth hazelnuts, gnarly walnuts and shiny chestnuts. 'Thank you,' I all but whispered. 'Tell me, you are not from around here, are you?'

'I pass through from time to time. I prefer this woodland track to the roadway.'

Was it as simple as that? This man was just travelling from one place to another and I happened to meet him on his way? 'You are not Dobunni, I think.'

'I am not. But the tribes must work together as one, so they must. I've fought side by side with the Dobunni. I will do again.'

'What brings you to roam through here?'

'There are many places these roads lead to. A *world* outside this village.'

'Do you search for the relics of St Alban?' I winced at myself for asking such a question out loud when it should have stayed only in my head.

Holding my gaze, he seemed to be considering me in a new light. 'These *relics* are for fools, they are.' He spat. 'We should be ready for war. It is coming, sooner than you know. It is *men* that win battles, sword edges that cut down, the strength of your arm, and the wits in your mind. They are the things we should value.' He breathed in and his nostril flared. 'You are not a boy to remain tilling the fields and reaping the harvest – *you* have a sharp edge, a hunger for more than you find here. God knows, you do not thrive. You need meat on your bones and purpose to feed your mind. You need the world beyond to shape you, so you do.'

'I do not plan to stay. Someday I will leave and be a warrior like you.'

'Then we had better get some sword practice in, lad.' He was off his horse, sword unsheathed in a moment, smiling.

I put down the nuts and took the sword once again, gripping it tightly under its weight. Wielding it as he had shown me, stepping and lunging.

'I see you have practised!'

'But a stick is not the same, the weight and balance of this sword is very different.'

'Now. Two hands to block downwards. Above your head, then bring it down hard but do not hit the ground.'

I did as he said. I did it again and again. He showed me other moves and found two sticks and we sparred.

The encounter reminded me my future lay with King Aurelius, beyond the village and the safety of what I knew. Did I have it in me to be a warrior? To fight in the war that was surely coming?

**

I told Mother the nuts were from Father Faustus, though I had not seen the old monk since the day I had asked him about the casket. I regretted being rude to him especially when the monks had been so generous. But my suspicion tainted my regard for him and heightened my fear for the monastery, especially with the talk of spies about.

I decided to share the nuts with old Veryan Hen. He had grown so frail. I tucked his felt blanket around him in his chair, and roasted the chestnuts on a shovel propped up over his fire. I was always drawn to him when I needed answers. He had lived among kings and understood the games of power.

'I've seen the Red Horseman again. Is he Calchwynedd? If he's just travelling through, where does he go and what does he do?'

'We live by a good road that brings folk to and from Glevum, many have business that you or I might never know.' As usual he gave nothing away.

'Do you think he's a spy for Cadrawd?'

Veryan Hen looked at me, the direct gaze that made me uncomfortable. 'Do you think it likely?' This evasion made me certain he knew something.

'No. I first saw him so long ago, before ever the talk of the relic, or even spies, began... I've spoken to him. He's... kind. But his accent is strange, he's not from anywhere around here. And you know he has little more faith in the relic than *you*.' Veryan Hen raised an eyebrow, a gleam in his eye. 'He said *relics are for fools*.'

'Perhaps he's right. But it does not matter; the relic is lost.'

I steeled myself and confided my suspicion that the gold casket holding the Relic of St Alban was hidden somewhere at the monastery. I trusted him entirely and the worry of it lifted from me. The old man stared at the fire, his expression unchanged.

'You're not surprised, are you?'

'Few things are surprising at my time in life. Least of all anything that pious and fanatical old monk might be up to. But you suppose he would keep the relic from Aurelius and Cadrawd because he believes them unworthy?'

'Yes, exactly. Does he know of the past, of Aurelius' attempt to kill the Saxon child?'

'He may, he may not. It was not widely spoken of.'

'He wants Aurelius to repent, and return to the obedience of God's laws. He thinks that without true faith, the relic would be useless in Aurelius' hands. He said it is sacred, and not the plaything of kings.'

'...Or monks?'

'He said that if Aurelius truly followed God's laws, the relic may be *revealed* to him.'

'Well, whatever the old goat is up to... it is not your concern or mine. All we know is his kindness in our need. The monks have been charitable which makes a change from their sermonising. I would advise that you stay out of Faustus' affairs. This casket you speak of may not even be the one. More trouble than you can imagine may be unleashed. There is danger in it either way.' He closed his eyes and pulled the felt blanket close about him. 'Put another log on the fire on your way out.'

I stood outside his hut for a moment. A swift movement entered the side of my vision, a crack of a twig. A shadow darted away. A slight limp. The tall poplars and pines obscured the dark form. Kennan?

Had he heard any of our talk?

19

'We must talk, you and I,' Mother said, her voice husky from coughing. She tucked her needle into her stitching and placed it carefully on the table. 'Luca, you have grown. The time has come for you to leave. You must go to Glevum and take your place with your king.'

'Why now?'

'You are not a child anymore. You are the same age as I was when I came here. You have a future waiting for you.'

Doubts knotted themselves in my belly.

'Mother, I am afraid.' I could not look at her. 'I know I must. I want to… But, King Aurelius said I'm to come when I'm grown fat and strong. Look at me, I'm thinner than a grass snake.' I used the words of the Red Horseman and they had good effect.

'Oh, Luca. I know. I have spoken with your father, and you are to have the same portion as Kennan. But that cannot stop you.'

'And he said I must fight, but I've no proper skill…'

'You fight all the time!' She almost laughed.

'Not with a sword.'

'Swords are only given to those who prove themselves worthy, you'll be taught if there is need. Enough of all this. What you have is what few others possess, the gift of the written words.'

'I can read and Father Faustus has taught me well, but is it enough? I know little of the world beyond here… How am I to serve him? What will he ask of me?'

'You must do your duty to the Dobunni. You're clever and will find a way to be useful. Aurelius is old. Who knows what will happen when he is gone? But you must be there ready to be a part of the future king's court.'

I blinked back tears. She touched my cheek.

'Stay until summer.' She softened. 'Build up your strength. Then you must go, my son.'

I thought of Lucanus. 'I am good at the pottery. Kennan prefers to work the fields and hunt. Does Father not need me?'

'Kennan can make pots too, perhaps not with the same… *elegance* as you. Your father has always known someday you will go. He will not stand in your way.' She took a breath, tilted her head to one side. 'I must ask more of you, Luca. You have more influence over your brother and sister than you realise; you must not draw them into conflict with your father. Promise me. You'll be gone, but they will need him.'

'I have no influence over Kennan.' I frowned. How she could think so? 'And it's Father who draws conflict with me,' I said sharply. 'Is it he who pushes me to go? I know I'm the cuckoo in his nest.'

'Cuckoo?' She looked aghast. I held her gaze, watching the slow realisation that I knew. The silence was long and awkward but I did not avert my eyes. 'How do… Who told you?'

'I worked it out.'

'How long have you known?' Her voice was little more than a whisper.

'Since Ario. Father Faustus keeps a chronicle, it's a record of—'

'I know what a chronicle is,' she snapped. 'I have not always been a potter's wife in this back end of beyond! Who else knows?'

'I've told no-one... I've kept it inside so long. But I must know—'

'Luca!' She stood up. 'Don't judge me, I was young.' She gasped as she spoke and reached for the edge of the table. 'Life was not like it is here. My own mother had died and I was influenced by the goings on around me. I fell in love, but, well...'

'With who? Who is my real father?'

I waited, watching the edge of her mouth as it twitched.

'...It all went wrong when my father was murdered...' She stopped and looked down, leaning on the table.

'Tell me, please. Tell me everything. How was he killed?'

'It was a fight, a terrible fight. I was there, I saw it. I went to him, my knees sliding in the warm slick of his blood as he took his final breath. When Aurelius came, he stood over him, his loyal friend, and roared out his anger. I shall never forget...'

She sat and rubbed her hands down her lap, soothing her discomfort.

'...I was left entirely alone. It is a credit to the king that he took charge of my fate, though when I began to show I was with-child I stayed out of his way. But then I was called before him. I was so afraid. I could no longer conceal what was obvious. I expected to be outcast. But to my surprise, I was called before him because Lucanus had requested my marriage. The king took one look at me and did not hide his relief to oblige, making the promise that my child would learn the writing for the sake of Atto whom he had loved above all others.'

'But the man you loved... he abandoned you? Did he even know of me?' She did not reply, but a silver tear streaked down her face. 'I'm sorry, Mother. I know you've done the best for me, for all of us...' I hated to make her sad, but so close to the truth I had to know. 'Who *is* he? My father?'

She turned away. 'There is nothing good that came from that time – except you. You are the light from the darkest of days. Lucanus is the only father you need. He has raised you and that is enough. The time is coming for you to follow your own path as I prepared you for. I've done everything I can to make sure you have the opportunity to make your own way.'

'Is it someone from the king's court?'

She began to cough. Guiding her to the stool, I held her shoulders until the fit passed. She would never tell.

'I ask that you make your peace with Kennan and set aside your differences with Lucanus,' her voice a croak though her words were clear. 'You have a bitter seed inside you; I must take much of the blame myself. I believe his harshness comes from… from my not returning his love… completely. He has taken it out on you at times.'

'Well, he is not an easy man to love!'

'Luca, you must understand. Lucanus offered me a way out, he's given me the best he could, but… I'm not like the other women in the village…'

'You are better than *any* of them.'

She smiled sadly. 'My son, you have the heart of a lion. I know you will make me proud at the king's court.'

'King Aurelius spirals into a state of ill health.' Lucanus brought news from Glevum. 'He barely sleeps or eats. They say he shouts and rants, at anyone and everyone for days at a time, until his voice becomes a whisper. He hacks out heart-wracking spit that leaves flecks of red blood in his white beard. He's gaunt and shrunken in height. They say, he's dying from the inside out. His need for the relic has never been greater, to secure the safety of us all. The search for it is now his sole and ruthless purpose.'

'But after all this searching, can it ever be found?' Minura asked.

'Who knows? But there is also talk that Cadrawd of the Calchwynedd has planted a scout watching this area. With this new desperation to find it, we must be on our guard. Desperate men are dangerous.'

We were at the final edge of winter but the cold ground hardened once more. Even the wildcats left the safety of the woodland to stalk the edges of the village in search of food – but these were not the only predators to arrive. Hoof beats sounded a dull, thudding drum beat, faint at first and too many to play out a rhythm. A dozen horses with well-dressed riders cantered onto the frosty village green. Skipping and snorting, they were as unsettled as the armed men they carried: King Aurelius' loyal soldiers. One man blew a horn, a summons to all. The villagers emerged from their huts, curious if not obedient.

'We come looking for spies and information,' rasped a middle-aged man, his voice like a blade on a grindstone. The cold air misted as it carried his words. 'Your duty is to King Aurelius and loyalty to him will be rewarded. BUT...' Over the general muttering and nodding he continued, 'But men of Calchwynedd have been in these parts. Men with no business to be trespassing under the nose of King Aurelius. No tolerance for spies, harbourers of spies, or concealment of items of interest to the king, will be permitted.'

He paused as more villagers gathered, Kennan and Vannii among them. Looking around, I knew every face, every name, and each person's business. What secrets they would find here I could not imagine.

Small children ran about scared as the agitated horses shifted uncomfortably. One little boy ran to his mother as a soldier nudged his horse towards him. The boy squealed and lurched into her arms out of harm's way. I looked at the soldier's smirking face; it was one of the Anderferas boys, Madoc, the skinny lad we had fought at the market. He must have found position among Aurelius' men.

'Your homes will be searched,' continued the spokesman. 'Anyone with information useful to the king may come forward… DISMOUNT.'

All the men prepared for their work. Their leader demanded trestles and a board to make up a table, while others began herding the villagers into groups. Each person was to be inspected and questioned.

It was cold. We were made to stand about. The quiet obedience soon became outraged indignation. Homes were not just searched, but looted and damaged, meagre possessions thrown out onto hard ground in the haste of discovery.

Nothing was discovered. Nothing at all.

We were poor people who could barely survive from one winter to the next. They did not find what they looked for, but appeared to be greatly enjoying the search. I was shepherded into a line with the rest. A miserable row of drab peasants with pinched faces, clutching their cloaks about them, rubbing hands and stamping feet. I stood, waiting for my turn to be questioned. At last, I approached the table. The man with the rasping voice cleared his throat as he had many times.

'Name. Point to whichever is your hut.' With barely a chance to answer, he looked up at me, his squinted expression, a judging, measuring stare. 'Anything to report?'

'Nothing.'

I moved away. The word *nothing* was repeatedly muttered, so when someone answered *yes*, there was a subdued hush to listen.

'I saw a stranger in these parts,' someone was saying. 'Riding on a horse with red bridle and cloak. Didn't see him close as he was up on the ridgetop. I guessed he must be something to do with the monastery, but he seemed to be just watching. Made me uneasy.'

'When was this?'

The voice was drowned out by the murmurs; I tried to move nearer to hear. Others also admitted seeing him; a suspicious character that must be found and interrogated. I felt sick. I could not believe the Red Horseman, that strange and mysterious figure who shadowed my life, was a spy.

I looked around at the mess about me. The village had not looked like this since the flood. I noticed Kennan in conversation with Vannii. They looked my way. Kennan caught my eye but turned his back. They were talking about me. After the searching and questioning was nearly over, and people were attempting to clear away their ransacked belongings, Vannii approached one of the soldiers. I watched as he was led away to the leader.

The starlings gathered in black dancing clouds, the geese flew in giant arrows across the sky, and new rumours surfaced, new sightings and new suspicions. I believe these stories to be flights of fancy, imagination enhanced by the drabness of our lives and the dire need for change to disrupt it.

Then news came from the monastery, the king had visited Father Faustus again.

King Aurelius' sickness had edged his desperation with vitriol, his patience run out. Father Faustus was tied to a cart and beaten on the soles of his feet with a nailed bat. He admitted nothing and they found nothing.

When I reached the monastery, I found pale pages of parchment skimming across the yard like dead leaves, monks chasing after them. Trunks and crates were broken and upturned, the wooden cross thrown into the low scraggy beech hedge and Crab was nowhere to be seen. The monks gave details in torrents of muttered outpourings. All too confused and frightened to reason it out.

One of the monks led me into a small hut where Father Faustus lay with his legs raised in blood-soaked bandages. He did not look at me. I was not sure he realised I was there. Another monk was changing the dressing, and peeled away the dripping red cloth to reveal fleshy ribbons that no longer resembled feet. He clumsily bound them as the old monk winced and gasped. Faustus would not walk again. Aurelius, the sly old devil, had targeted only his feet, still believing that the monk might be useful to him.

'I'm surprised *you* are come.' He seemed annoyed but perhaps it was the terrible pain.

'Let me bring Veryan Hen to you, let him mix up a salve for your wounds...'

'No, you'll not,' he snapped, still looking away. 'I'll not have that *pagan* in here with his potions.' Crab emerged from behind him at the sound of my voice.

'Crab, you alright?' I asked, knowing I would get no answer. He tilted his head and looked sad, but had no injury to show me. He squeezed my elbow, afraid. I touched his shoulder and nodded to show I understood. He had few friends, and none but me beyond the monastery gate. We both knew other monasteries had been burned to the ground, the monks all killed.

'Someone,' Faustus looked at me at last, 'has spread a rumour about this place.'

I immediately understood – he thought it was me. But surely, he could not believe that I had said anything to anyone. 'What rumour? Who would...?'

'I thought *you* might tell me.' The old monk stared into me. The light in the hut was dim but I glimpsed a teary gleam in his eye.

'But I've not heard anything.' There was a silence. We both knew what he meant. 'I've not said anything, why would I?'

Faustus sighed. 'Someone has suggested to Aurelius that I have concealed the relic.'

'But who would… do you have any enemies?' I asked.

'Have you?' he asked, with that stare down his nose.

Nagging fears were curling into a nook in my mind. I had trusted Veryan Hen, though Faustus clearly did not. There was silence between us.

'I've done much in my life,' his anger turned to sadness, 'that might lead men to hurt me, but none that I can think would construct such a… fabrication about me.

'Crab, see to the fire, I'm frozen,' Father Faustus snapped. I felt a chill myself, was this my doing? My guilt at being any cause of the trouble, sat like cold lead in my stomach. But I would never give up Father Faustus for any reward for the relic. He was so knowledgeable and clever. Whatever he had or had not done, it was not for me to question his judgement.

'Aurelius has not found it, but is convinced I have it… He'll be back… or others will.'

20

I sat beside Kennan on the cart. I had promised our mother that I would make peace with him. I tried. A few words had sprung between us without anger, and as the yellow buds of prickly gorse flowered the toleration became something close to cooperation. We were off to Glevum, to market. Just the two of us.

'Curse my back, that I cannot manage it myself,' Lucanus had grumbled. 'I've no choice but to leave it to you two mochyns.' His voice deeper these days, his words sliding out gruff and grainy, sometimes slurring one into another. 'Luca, you're the oldest, if you mess this up I'll thrash you like never before. If you argue or fight each other I'll string you up by your boots.'

I thought he was finally showing his approval and trust, but then he had added, 'We can't eat coins. Come back with food or tools.' It was a sting to my silver coin. It had more value than anything we owned – but only if someone wanted it. The Saxons might, but they would likely cut my throat for it. So, I had stitched it into the hem of my cloak.

The cart rumbled along the old Roman road. Our shoulders rubbed together as we left the village behind. We did not speak. Though, as we neared the old town, somehow the magic of Glevum began to settle between us and we were to find a trace of unity once again.

Spring had come earlier in Glevum. The dusty air was thicker, the hum and buzz was louder. Even before we reached the first row of columns and stone houses, the rumble of news emerged from the

147

town like bats from a roof hole – war had finally arrived.

The side streets were heaving as crowds jostled around backstreet weapon dealers. Kennan and I had a job to pitch the cart through it all. The smithies thronged with would-be soldiers with would-be weapons needing urgent transformation into deadly blades, hatchets, or spears, or even catapults and cudgels.

In contrast, the worn paving in the forum marketplace had an echo of emptiness as few traders were setting up for business, those that did were less concerned with the activity of the Jutes, and more concerned at the impact on trade for the day. We unpacked the pots but the excitement was infectious.

'Luca, the man over there says Cynric Claw-hand and his warriors are massing out on the Atrebates downs, shield-beating and roaring. He says, Saxons from the Gewisse are joining them, in greater number than ever before.'

'Well, I just heard Aurelius has declared King Cynric must be challenged and this unity with the Gewisse must be stamped on. Apparently, Aurelius has gone south to Badon, calling all men and women to take up arms of any kind and follow him.' Outraged and provoked, the Dobunni spirit for war raised its head.

'Should we go?'

It was in my mind too, we had revelled in the tales of battles and heroes, and this was our first chance for the real thing. Wasn't this where my destiny lay?

'What about all this?' I indicated to the cart: the pots, the pony, the expectation of bartered food and essentials.

'Yeah, I suppose… But I'd like to, wouldn't you?' We looked at each other for a long moment. 'Just leave it all, and go. We'll come back for it after.'

'There'll be nothing to come back to,' I laughed. 'It'll all be taken. That's if we come back at all.'

'You scared to die?'

'I'm more scared to live and to tell mother you died… and *either* way, you know Father would kill me.' It was said flippantly, but it was a truth we both recognised.

'Yeah, and if I returned without *you* Mother would never forgive me. You've always been her favourite.'

I was physically struck by this. Perhaps she found it easier to show love for me, I am like her. He is like Lucanus. Was this where the jealousy stemmed from? He let out a deep sigh. There was a warmth between us that had been gone a long time. This was the closest we had been since I scratched his pike onto the rock.

We did not go to war.

We set up the pots but few people remained, milling about but not filling the spaces. Certainly, the talk of those in the market was cynical of the outcome and critical of the leadership. '*Aurelius is too vain to organise an army,*' some said. '*He cares more about relics. Instead of creating divisions he should have been building allies,*' another said. '*He should've created a strategy and battle tactics. Few of those gone will return.*'

Despite the few customers, we did well. We bartered for pigs' trotters and ears, salted pilchards, a basket of mixed vegetables, cider, and a sack of dried peas.

'It's the wealthy with something to lose that have no appetite for battle,' Kennan said.

'And those with nothing are hungry for it.'

'You remember Madoc and the lad like a bull?'

'The Andeferas boys? They joined up with the king's men. Maybe someone persuaded them to fight for something worth fighting for.'

'Yeah, they've gone to fight now, I heard. Along with the other waifs and strays with little to live for.'

When the market was over, we left the stones and the gossip, the straight lines and statues, the rooftops and paving, and the smell of people, and trundled our way back along the rolling Roman road home.

Travellers from either direction spread news. The small rabble army that left Glevum had been overwhelmed. What began as a skirmish with a few Jutes on the borderlands became a slaughter as the Gewisse piled in. King Aurelius' son had been killed.

The promise of victory and the excitement of Glevum had sunk like rock in a rippling pool.

**

So, young Prince Coinmail had lost his father. My mother cried at the news as she stirred a broth of wood-pigeon and parsnip, the tears on her cheek lit by the cook fire.

'Did you know him?'

'Of course! I lived and worked in the royal household. He was just a little older than I. He once pulled my hair when I beat him in a race.' She smiled sadly. 'I kicked him in the knee and we became… friends.'

She had never spoken of him before. The question of my real father rose into my mouth. But I could not ask it. Was King Aurelius' son my father? Did Aurelius suspect that? Was that why he gave me the opportunity to learn at the monastery? Was that why she could never tell?

While the Jutes and Saxons threatened our borders, an invisible killer lurked among us. A venom that poisoned the blood and spread fast through the people of Framlutum, making them spit bubbling pink phlegm from deep within.

Minura, slight and suddenly frail, collapsed as I caught her, lighter than a minnow plucked from the cold stream. Her skin was damp with sweat, but without the warmth of the living. Her body convulsed with a retching cough, writhing in my arms, gasping for air.

Bellicia too. Maccus gave me the news. 'She clings to the linen cover, her dried and cracked lips burn red, and her hair sticks to her face in cold sweat.'

That moment I kissed her returned to me; her rain-wet curls stuck to her cheek, her darkened lashes framing her blue eyes, her wet body tight against mine.

Our small village was losing folk to the sickness. Swift and devastating. Old, young, fit or thin. There is no prejudice in death. Veryan Hen struggled to cope. I assisted him where I could, as did our mother though I feared for her as she tended those weak and sick. The winter had given little food and there was little ready so early in spring, but with death on the doorstep it is hard to swallow anyway. I did not see Maccus for a few days, and then heard that he had it too. Sulio also.

Checking on Minura one morning, I found her with eyes open, blinking and alert, her breath calm and returning to normal. I hugged her and carried her out into the winter sun. She squinted and smiled, weak but better. I wrapped a blanket about her and gave her a bowl of hot milky oats.

I went to see Maccus, or was it Bellicia? Maccus was at the coughing phase and did not register I was there. Bellicia was calm, asleep, much like Minura before she woke – and much like others before they died. I sat beside her. I stroked her arm.

All the complexities and hurt fell away as I looked at her closed dry lips, the slight shallow movement in her chest. I told her that she had made me happier than I had ever been, and that whatever happened I would always hold the memory of her like a treasured possession.

The next day she woke. She smiled weakly as I came to her. I pulled her into me and held her, warm with life. I carried her, lighter than she ought to have been, but a welcome burden in my arms. I took her to our hut where she sat with Minura. They held hands in the sunshine.

She turned Vannii away when he came to her. When she looked at me it was with the same desire that had been there before. She must have seen it in me, I could disguise it no longer. But life hindered us once again, in the cruellest way.

Our mother's coughing had lain dormant beneath the bloom of wellbeing. The sickness brought it back, this time erupting in retching and urging breathlessness. Small beads of sweat appeared on her brow, her black hair framing her white face. Kennan and I were forced together often in caring for her.

'It seems you boys have found a new peace.' Her voice was little more than a whisper. Her smile brightened her eyes though her lips were dry and cracked. I looked at Kennan and he looked at his feet. Despite the cold, she burned up in a fever one day then shivered the next. We stayed close to our roundhouse, busy with the washing and mending, the planting and picking, preparing food, and helping Minura to keep the home clean and provided for. Kennan kept the fire stoked and I steamed and mashed the food to mush to spoon feed our mother until she could no longer eat at all. I kept up this busyness and vigil over the long days.

I watched as she struggled for air. My knuckles white with clenching as I willed her to find it. Veryan Hen rubbed a salve over her chest and neck, smelling of cloves, juniper, and mint. Strain showed in her expression and in the tendons of her neck. Her agitated body convulsed again and again.

Then suddenly stopped.

She lay still, calm but empty of being.

Her eyelids deeply sunken, her skin fixed like a thin film of pale wax. But her hair, still smooth, black and flowing about her, was beautiful and alive as I arranged it over her shoulders. Her hands were cupped as if ready to give or receive something. I settled them together over her heart, the slight resistance to the movement indicating that the fluidity of life had gone.

Her secrets gone with her.

21

The only thing I had to fight the hurting of loss was anger.

I was angry with the sun. How dare it rise as if nothing had occurred? I was angry with the bean shoots. How dare they grow when she had gone? I was angry with the goose, the pig, and the cow; vividly alive, breathing the air as she should breathe. My anger spilled in a rage at the sky, the rocks, and the earth. I let out a demonic roar at the passing clouds. I brutally smashed at the boulders with small jagged stones until my bleeding hands could no longer hold them. My cheeks stung with tears as I cut and gouged at the ground as I dug out her grave alongside Kennan. We were united in our grief but were unable to meet the gaze of the other.

Without Mother the fire went out. The hearth became cold. We all suffered, I know that. In our different ways we were all lost. Minura did her best but Lucanus always found fault with her. I tended the spring vegetables, remaining close to the roundhouse to watch over my poor struggling sister.

Without Mother's clear wisdom and gentle pressure to restrain Lucanus' temper, the simmering tensions began to boil over. He scolded Minura: the meal was not cooked, the house was untidy, the washing was unclean. She sniffed back tears but one fell down her cheek, dropping so fast it left barely a trace. She was so thin, still weak from her own sickness. My fists clenched.

'Leave her alone.' I looked him straight in the eye. 'She's exhausted. Kindness instead of endless criticism might help.' I held his gaze. The skin below his eye twitched. He stared back at me uncertain, unnerved. Mother would have said something similar in her own subtle way. He blinked, unsure for a moment.

'Keep your mind on your own matters,' he snarled, 'and watch your tongue.'

'You should do more to help.' My tongue was on fire. 'You sit in the pottery so long then complain when things are not done.'

He stroked his beard. Eyes tiny and screwed. 'Luca, you're not too old or too big to be thrashed. I'll take my stick to your backside 'til it bleeds.'

'You treat Redak better than me,' I carried on with a scarcely concealed contempt. 'You give her more to eat too, yet you demand my obedience more than hers.'

I had beat Kennan with words but with Lucanus arguments were never allowed, violence always came first. Now, face to face with him, he did not know whether to argue or hit me. What if I fought him? He was so sturdy and broad, strong and severe. But he was not clever. Mother had said, '*Lucanus is the only father you need.*' But he never loved me. All his beatings resided under my skin. A rash waiting to flare up.

'Luca.' Kennan stormed in. 'Where is my knife? You used it last. You should put it back if you use it.'

'I never touched it.' Typical Kennan, now I was attacked from both sides. 'You used it to cut the twine on the fence post this morning.'

'JUST GIVE HIM HIS KNIFE, LUCA,' Lucanus bawled.

'I NEVER TOUCHED IT. You *always* take Kennan's side.' I recklessly willed the aggravation now started.

'Because you always think you're right about everything.'

'And when I am, still you take his side.'

'Oh, stop your complaining, and don't answer back.' He turned away, his big hands in tight fists.

But I had not finished. 'You've never let me have my say. You'll never hear my side of things.'

'Enough, Luca.'

'Enough? But I've not even begun...'

'ENOUGH.'

'It's always been the same. You assume the worst of me and deny me the chance tell my side: *don't speak, don't plead.* I took your thrashings without a sound or complaint, but you beat me anyway. You said I was lazy, but I was trying to get things right so you'd be satisfied. I spent my life wanting to please you, hoping for the kindness you showed Kennan, but you never showed any affection to me, even when we were small, you never made me feel safe and wanted as a father should.'

My breath was running out but more words were clamouring to be spoken. 'You made me fight against you, then beat me for doing it. You rejected my efforts. I *hate you.*'

He came lumbering towards me, his lips tight in a wordless outrage.

I dodged.

'You always blamed me for everything. You made me feel bad for learning at the monastery, but insisted I went. You demand my work in the pottery but tell me I'm useless.'

'LUCA.' He growled through his teeth like a bad-tempered wolf. 'I've warned you...' He was following me around the small hut. I was edging backwards, every step with every word. I had so much more to say.

'You blamed me for things that Kennan did, you punished me and not him. Nothing I did was ever good enough.'

We were out into the yard. His fist swung at me. He was easy to read, easy to dodge.

'You found fault with everything. When you might give me praise you just grunted, not one kind word, *ever*.'

'I gave you my home and provided for you all these years. I made sure you were fed and warm. But all I got in return was your unruly behaviour, and your sharp tongue and fists to your brother. You deserved every thrashing, and, my god, you will be thrashed now.'

'Unruly behaviour? You never understood what was happening right beneath your nose. Kennan's fists are as hard as mine, and more often the ones to start trouble.'

I forgot Kennan was there, but in the corner of my vision I saw the flick of his woollen tunic as he jumped the pig fence and left. Good.

Lucanus picked up a stick and swiped at me. I ducked just in time and swerved around him, grabbing the shovel I used to dig Mother's grave.

'Don't lay the blame on your brother. You're a toad, Luca. Leeching off me since the day you were born, bringing trouble and misery to your mother. You've gone too far. My god, I will punish you for this.'

My fingers tightened around the smoothed grain of the shovel handle, its weight and balance in both my hands. I swung it high.

It twisted as my arms rose and battered him with the flat of the blade on his head. The impact had jolted through me. He stumbled and roared. The reality of what I was doing choked my confidence. Had the shovel not twisted the blade would have lodged in his head and would surely have killed him.

Seizing my hesitation, his stick struck my ribs, winding me. He came at me, grabbing my tunic at the neck and squeezing his thick fist, I was lifted off my feet, a hard knuckle painfully lodged at my throat as I was pressed up against the side of the pottery shack.

'You're no longer welcome under this roof.' His warm spit

flecked my chin. But my fight and my anger remained. Tensing the muscles in my thigh, I drove my knee into his crotch.

Released, I stumbled as my feet hit the ground. I picked up the shovel again. I raised it once more but was grabbed from behind. Maccus and his father and two other men from the village had heard the trouble and come to stop it.

They steered me away, my fingers shaking with unfinished loathing.

'What will you do now, Luca?'

It was a question I had no good answer for. I was sat with Maccus and Bellicia.

The Red Horseman came to mind, a thin line of hope. I would find him and travel with him wherever it was he went. *I wish*. Really, there was only one option. 'Go to King Aurelius.'

'But, the *war*, Luca.' Bellicia looked worried. 'You will have to fight if you go.'

'I know. There is news of Jutes and Saxons all over. Last I heard, Aurelius is building an army in Badon.'

'Will you join it? Become a warrior?'

'I must. I can learn.'

'But what's all the purpose of those hours at the monastery,' Maccus said, 'only to die in a fight? You'd be no use to Aurelius dead.'

'Well, it's surely not to become a monk!' Bellicia laughed. We all laughed and the friendship eased my mind.

'But, right now, it's fighters that he needs, I've no idea what other use I might be.'

'A scribe, a clerk maybe?'

'A spy, you'd make a good spy.'

I looked at Bellicia, surprised. 'Why would you say that?' But they both laughed again.

'It's just, well… you have eyes like a bird of prey – intelligent and watchful. You see things others wouldn't notice. You're quiet and sharp…'

'And reckless,' Maccus cut in.

'When will you go?'

'Soon. My mother said I should go this summer, and I'll not stay under the same roof as Lucanus.'

'You must stay here, with us.'

'No. It would be awkward for your family. I'd not want to draw any of you into my troubles.'

'But things are better with Kennan these days, aren't they?'

'To be honest I'm not sure. We've had moments when things are better but it could change any time. Even now, after fighting Lucanus, he will hate me again.'

'Brothers. One minute you're trying to kill each other, the next best friends.' Maccus shook his head.

He had known us all our lives, seen us wrestle and fight, and been witness to the jealous and competitive squabbles and injuries. Yet he still assumed we must be close. I realised how much Kennan and me had grown used to the pretence that we liked each other, when in fact we no longer did. The closeness I found in Glevum was less about brotherly affection and more a sad realisation that the gulf between us stretched right back to the beginning. Lucanus favoured Kennan. Mother favoured me. We were physically close when we were young; his shoulder nudging against mine and that feeling of the world being out of balance when the heat of him was not at my side. Was that the true bond of brotherhood? Even with the insecurity and jealousy that was already there at that time?

'I'll speak with him, help him understand, and try to make peace between you.' My silence must have made Maccus rethink.

'He once swore to kill me, you know. I actually think one day he will.'

'So,' Bellicia touched my arm and changed the direction. 'You will stay with us. There's much work to be done now the winter is left behind, the ploughing and calving...'

'Yes, stay with us, at least help sow the fields. The villagers would be glad of it. Many have lost so much this last year.'

'You're right, I owe it to the village to help, but then I *must* go... I must take my chances.'

'But Aurelius can be cruel.' Bellicia looked concerned for me. '...What he did to Father Faustus...'

'I'll never forget that. But don't worry about me. There's something else though... Promise me you'll look out for Minura. I know you will, Bellicia, but Mac... Maybe it's too much to ask, but Kennan will never step in if Lucanus is cruel. Now my mother is gone, she'll do all the work and—'

'Of course, don't worry about that. I'll always be here for her.' He looked embarrassed. I had been too caught up in my own troubles to notice but, Minura was growing up, and pretty. A good match for the gentle Maccus. I looked at Bellicia. She was looking away.

'You'll not come back, will you?' She could have been speaking to the air.

I knew what she meant. Would I come back for her? There was no answer to this. My life was precarious, unpredictable and loose, my certainties vanished.

'Luca.' Maccus changed the subject. 'There's a stag in the east pine-woods. Sulio found the trail. We're going to hunt for it, the gang like old times… Come with us.'

'Maccus I…'

'Maybe this'll help with Kennan. It'll be something… outside of the village and your usual feuding.'

I had to admit, the best times between Kennan and me had been away from the homestead, thrown together where our differences were pushed down the scale of importance. But Vannii too?

'We'll go, like the old days,' Maccus persuaded. 'We'll kill a stag.' He was excited about the idea, and it was infectious though my instinct resisted. The gang. I had not been part of the gang for years. I doubted they would want to include me. I was not sure this hunt that Maccus was so keen to relive was wise.

'Please, Luca. A stag! Have one last adventure with me before you leave.' There was an intensity in my friend's eyes. It was a genuine request from the heart. 'The others often ask after you. You should join us… They'll be glad to share one last hunt with you, leave with a good memory behind you.'

I had tasted stag a few times, there was no better meat. Memory of the flavour rose to my mouth with the warm water of hunger.

'Don't leave here with trouble as your last memory,' Maccus

added. '…Or you'll definitely not come back.'

Stag meat. Maccus. That was two good reasons to set our differences aside for a day or two. I nodded and he hugged me. I smiled, happy.

The next day we toiled late in the fine spring air, driving the plough blade, row after row, turning the dry surface soil over into long lines of earth. Sulio and Goliath were friendly enough but Vannii was another matter. He joined us as we sat in the sun, sweat and dust drying on our skin.

'Heard you tried to kill your father.'

'He's not my father.'

'Well…'

I took pleasure in seeing Vannii awkward.

'I suppose it was brave to take him on.'

I recognised that he was trying to be friendly, though I knew Maccus had put him up to it. His fake smile lingered a moment too long, and I knew he would rather spit in my food. My trust was not soothed, but my spirits were. I would go on the hunt.

22

'Evening, young Luca. Come in sit down, I have something for you.'
The old man handed me a worn deer-hide bag. 'It's old. It was given
to me when I first left my home and my family, so many years past;
re-stitched and repaired countless times.' Veryan Hen already knew I
was leaving.

'Thank you… It'll need a further repair along the side seam, a
task I'll be glad to do.' Holding the worn leather bag, I imagined the
places and adventures the bag had been part of and excitement
about leaving tingled inside me for the first time.

'There is a story I must tell you before you go.'

I sat down, watching him, saying nothing. 'You know that I
served King Aurelius… but then I met my wife, she was the healer
in these parts back then. My time was split between Glevum and
her. She taught me the herbs and the remedies… but not how to
dispel her own sickness.'

I knew all this, I waited for more.

'I regret not spending more time with my love when I had the
chance.' His old eyes gleamed with tears that did not spill. 'Glevum
drew me in to its intrigue and affairs but, now I look back… much of
it all is best forgotten. But there is one matter that must be recalled.'

He paused, leaving me curious.

'The world is built on the private lives of us all. Secrets, and the
consequences of them, must sometimes be shared. This was never
my secret to reveal, but now… well, things change.' He settled back

into his chair. I perched on the very edge of my stool.

'I told you of the plot to kill the Gewisse child, Ceawlin? There are details of that tale I left untold. In the last days I served Aurelius, I was already old and overdue a peaceful retirement, but that is when I met the man you know as the Red Horseman.'

'I knew it! You always turned my questions onto something else. So, tell me now, what do you know?'

The old man twisted his head further and smiled. 'Like I said, this was never my secret to reveal, but it's a relief to tell you at last, boy. The man is known to me as *the Jay*...'

'The Jay?' I pictured his black dropping moustache, much like the markings of a jay bird, and the blue-black feathers he threaded into his hair with beads.

'...You remember the High King of the western hills, Brochfael of the Tusks, sent a spy to watch over Aurelius? Fearing his schemes may bring further trouble with the Jutes and the Gewisse?'

I nodded and sat back to listen, his voice filling my mind.

'That spy was the Jay. A mysterious man who played beautiful music on a lyre, but in winning the trust of Aurelius he also caught the eye of a young maid. Realising her father was Aurelius' chief steward, he began to spend time with her to get access to the information he sought. They met in secret and as the May buds blossomed the two fell in love.'

'You mean Atto. You mean... my *mother*?' I was surprised and yet not at the same time.

'She told him she was expecting a baby.'

'Me?'

'He resolved to take her back to the far western hills of his home. He promised her a life in the court of the High King, a life of status and fine things. Seeking her father to ask for her hand, he came across Aurelius' men talking over a parchment, a map outlining the plot – undeniable proof of the intent to kill Ceawlin. It was the evidence he needed. In an opportune moment he stole it.'

'Did my mother know of this?'

'She was about to find out, in the cruellest way. The Jay rushed to her home, to bid her to fly away with him there and then. But Atto, realising what he was up to, followed him. Finding him with his daughter, there was a confrontation. Atto was killed.'

'My grandfather was killed *by the Jay*?' No wonder my mother would never speak of my real father. She had told me how her knees had slid in the warm slick of her father's blood and how Aurelius had roared out his anger.

'The Jay was chased through the town, into the fields and over the hills, but they never found him. He returned to his homeland a broken man. He gave the incriminating parchment to Brochfael of the Tusks. It was too late to stop the attempt, but as we know, Aurelius' plot ended in failure. And without Atto… these were dark days indeed.'

The old man stopped speaking. My mind caught up with the words he had spoken. I was holding my breath. 'The Red Horseman!' I finally gasped. 'The Jay, is my father!'

'He came to me when he heard your mother had died.' The old man reached out and touched my knee. 'He requested I tell you the truth of your birth. He wants to offer you a place in his home.'

The strange Red Horseman, who had always connected with something deep inside me, was the man who killed my grandfather. And he had done so to save the baby Gewisse prince, Ceawlin. And in doing so, had never known his own child, me. Had my mother *truly* loved the Jay? There had been a sadness in her. Did she ever forgive him?

'So, is he good, or bad? I cannot make it out.'

'Luca, have I not always taught you? Things are never so simple.

For my mind, he means well… but to Aurelius he was the enemy. And your mother, well…'

'How long have you known all this?'

'Much of it I guessed, some your mother hinted at. The Jay filled in the rest, though it's the look of you that made me certain, you've grown very like him. And not *just* in looks I might add.'

'Did my mother love him, I mean, still?'

'She is not here to say, and I cannot know. But the horror of her father's death hardened her heart for years. Before she died, she told me she had made peace with the past.'

She told me she had not loved Lucanus *completely*. Perhaps she kept a place in her heart for the Jay after all. 'The Red Horseman – the Jay, where is he now? How do I find him?'

'The light is fading fast, the night is upon us, he may be gone, but you could look on the knoll. If he has gone, then mend the bag and bide your time…'

I was at the threshold in a step.

'Luca, say nothing to anyone… It is not wise to worsen matters with Lucanus, and by association, taint your mother's memory with gossip.'

I nodded and left.

**

I raced up to the knoll where I had first seen him on his white horse. He was not there. Then through the gloom of the trees, I spotted the crimson flash of his cape. He was waiting for me.

'I hoped you would come. You have seen the old man?'

'I have, he has told me.' My insides churned like the writhing of snakes inside me. 'It's dangerous for you here,' I said, though I was so glad that he was. 'There is talk of you, they suspect you're Cadrawd's spy.'

'It is not the first time.' He smiled but it faded fast from his face. He stepped close. 'I'm sorry.' He shook his head. 'I broke your mother's heart... She broke mine, so she did. I searched for her everywhere. I never stopped loving her... When I finally found her *here*... she had other children... and the hope of being with her ended. I contented myself with a glimpse of her. Of you.'

My eyes warmed and watered. It was tragic. The loss for both him and my mother moved me. He reached out and gripped my shoulder. The firmness of his touch making it all so real.

'The few meetings with you gave me hope... that we may not live as complete strangers.' Though the dusk of evening made it hard to see, our eyes met and connected. 'Luca, can I embrace you as a father? I have waited many years.'

I stood still as he folded his arms around me. I wanted this, but I stiffened: this was the man who had murdered Atto. His arms were strong, yet there was a tenderness in his hold. I could not resist. I let my armour fall away and returned the embrace. I finally knew what a father's love felt like. Not strangers.

'There's a place for you in my home,' he said, pressing his forehead to mine, his warm hands cradling my head as if to take me into his heart. And I'll teach you to fight.' He drew back and smiled. 'You can at last take your place at my side, so you can. And serve Brochfael of the Tusks, Lord of Powys. If you want it…'

'Yes! Yes, I do. I'll be glad to.'

'You know the Jutes and Gewisse have been gathering this last month. There's been skirmishes and raids.'

'Yes, and the king's son is dead.'

'A great loss. A tragedy for the future of the Dobunni.'

'You knew him?'

'A man I knew… from a distance, shall we say, and who would have been a *better* king someday soon. He was brave to be sure. Braver than his father, of that there's no doubt.

'But Aurelius has gone to fight too—'

'Aurelius will never go into battle. He lives in fear of Cynric Claw-hand. He knows that he would be personally targeted by Cynric's fiercest dogs.'

'He'll stay in Badon?'

'A large army has been assembling in Badon. Men from many of the tribes have joined it.'

'You go to join it?'

'I do. Men from Dumnonia will fight alongside Dobunni and my countrymen too.'

'And Cadrawd? Will all the Britons be united?'

'Cadrawd is all but cut off and would be a fool to risk leaving the Calchwynedd unguarded. The scouts say Cynric is moving to take the old hillfort of Sarum. He must be stopped.

'Let me come with you—'

'No, boy. You've developed your skill but have much to learn. You have a fighter's heart but you have more than that and... and I have plans for you. I have only just begun to be a father to you. I'll not risk losing you now. Wait for me.'

'Please, let me come. Let me fight with you.'

'Luca, this fight will be hard to win. The word is that Cynric has paraded his son, Ceawlin, among the Jutes as the living proof of a prophecy that is being fulfilled. This prince of the Gewisse is only a few months older than you but he's already become a trained warrior, and Cynric has schooled him in the dirty tricks of war, feeding him hatred for us Britons.'

'Veryan Hen has told me of this. It's why everyone is so desperate for the relic of St Alban to be found.'

The Jay spat in distaste. 'If I ever come across this relic of St Alban I will destroy it, so I will. It's brought nothing but trouble.' Perhaps he saw my look as he went on. 'Aurelius only wants it for his own glory. He forgets how to make his people safe... Anyway, enough of this talk.' He dismissed the matter with a wave of a gloved hand. 'I will return. Wait for me.'

'But how long? It is dangerous for you too.'

'Do not fear for me. I *will* return. The battle is imminent, if I do not hurry, I will miss it!' He smiled. 'Bide here and I will come for you as soon as I can.'

'I would rather come with you and fight than wait here.'

'Luca, say your farewells. Old Veryan will fetch you. Be ready.'

23

The Jay, the elegant horseman and warrior of Powys, had plans for me. I would have a new life in the shadow of my *father*. My feet trod firmer over the ground and my head bobbed light with optimism. I looked forward to the stag hunt. Maccus was right, I would leave with a good memory of friendship. Nothing Kennan or Vannii did mattered to me now.

We met early. The morning air was sharp but dry. Birds sang in the dawn light and our steps sounded a melody. We traipsed with laughter at foolish doings of the past, skipping over sour memories that might taint the new ones; Kennan and I were passively ignoring each other as we were so accustomed to do. Through beech woods and damp alder groves, we set out just as we had six years earlier when we hunted the boar. This time with Redak, bounding ahead, nose to the ground, zigzagging and weaving through uncoiling ferns.

Maccus lent me a bow and I had made arrows. The flights were white feathers, a rare find from an owl. The long shafts in my belt gave a nudging reminder of stag meat. I was pleased with the arrows and hoped they would bring me a kill.

Reaching the bluebell grove, sunlight pierced through the delicate new leaves unfurling above in fluorescent green, as the dark trunks reached up from the blue carpet spread before us. A stream caught the light, creating a silver divide. We traced its route, leading us deeper into the forest.

It had become a habit to collect plants on the way. I noted every detail of new buds, catkins, and fungi, which would please old Veryan

Hen. The others mocked me, scratching about in the dirt and gathering like a squirrel. This time, I enjoyed the humour it brought.

I found Death Cap mushrooms.

'Those are edible,' said Vannii.

'No. They're very poisonous, they'll make you so sick you'll want to die. Your throat swells so you can't breathe.'

'How do you know that if they kill you?' asked Sulio.

'Luca just likes to impress us, but he makes it all up.' Vannii was not going to let me be right. 'I've had them before.'

'You going to eat one then?' I challenged him with a smile, keeping the animosity at bay.

'Yeah, but not now.' He turned away and Maccus changed the talk to something else.

We were nearly at the thick pine-woods, to the east edges where the stag was first spotted. We hoped to find the deer before the fawns were born. Once they had young in the herd, they would be more aggressive and nervous. We reached the denser trees and knew we were getting close. The damp smell of earth and perfumed pine grew thicker as we moved, slowly climbing uphill. The day was drawing out. This was not a trail I had taken before.

'The birchwood joins this somewhere soon.' Sulio was confident in his direction. 'That'll be the best site to check first for deer.' We trekked on, the ground still rising. I spotted rowan and juniper buds amongst the straight pines, clues to our way.

'We're close to the birchwoods now?' I asked. Sulio smiled and nodded his head. Within a few paces the light changed and the mass of scrubby birch loomed over the uplands.

'We'll follow it back towards the setting sun. Keeping the pines on the left and the birch on the right. Go slow and quiet.' I liked the way Sulio took charge.

Movement against the jagged mass of branches caught my eye; the fine antlers of a stag slowly revolved in our direction, revealing the great head of a fine beast. Keeping still, we strained to see the red coats of others, their heads down, grazing on the fresh tree seedlings the spring forest offered in the cool evening. We watched them as *hunters*, not boys thrashing about with little idea. We all drew back, whispering a plan as Kennan held Redak by the thick ruff of her neck.

'We'll circle them from this side, it's downwind. Take your time and go silent. They won't be inclined to roam far this time of day, they're too busy grazing the new shoots.' We nodded at Sulio.

'Don't take a shot, unless it's sure.' Maccus always stuck to the hunter's code, I admired him for that. 'Aim for the heart. The best shot is from the side, at an angle, aim just behind the foreleg. Not the guts, it's a slow death – if it doesn't feel right let the shot pass.' Again, we all nodded, and stood up. Maccus touched Kennan's arm. 'And be sure to keep Redak behind.'

'Oh, one more thing…' added Sulio. 'When we surround them, watch out for each other, a miss might fly at one of us opposite.'

We all nodded again. I thought of Kennan's arrows on the boar hunt so many years before. I caught his eye. Our gaze held for a moment. I cannot say what he was thinking, nor for that matter, what was in my own mind.

We fanned out. Goliath and Kennan went furthest to approach from the birchwood side. Maccus and Vannii would come in from behind, while Sulio and I crept slowly through the pines. Silently inching through the underbrush, keeping the trees in line to hide us, we moved in.

I crouched. Rising slowly, I lifted my bow. My thighs burned as I remained still. With my arrow nocked ready, I took aim at the fine stag, its magnificent head raised and turned away from me. I aimed for the back of the neck.

Then I saw the pale streak of Goliath's arm ahead. I passed at the shot, not confident my aim would be true. The stag lowered his head to graze once more, stepping slowly onwards. Half crouching again, I silently side-stepped along with it. It raised its head again, perhaps sensing movement from the birchwood as it looked that way, giving me another opportunity for a shot. I raised my arrow, the burning in my thighs causing a tremor in my leg. I closed one eye, and took aim.

Kennan stood directly opposite; his arrow aimed at the stag too.

Or was it at me?

The stag forgotten. We eyed each other down the shaft of our arrows.

I lowered mine. Holding my gaze at him.

I heard the munching of the deer, bark tearing, a scuff of hoofs and tail flicking. Kennan also lowered his bow. The deer moved forward. I side-stepped alongside it once more.

I heard the twang of a bow string.

The stag reared up with a scream of hot air misting around its mouth.

We chased. The forest filled with sounds. There was movement on all sides. I could not see where the beast was hit, it stumbled as it ran. It began to slow. I slowed. It stopped. I stopped. I could not get a shot to the heart, but the neck was clear. It was injured and we must kill it fast.

I aimed and loosed my arrow straight at the thick neck. It skimmed the coarse hair, a terrible shot.

We were running again. My second shot hit. Someone else's too. But the great lithe beast kept going. After some distance it began to drag its hind legs, its front determined not to give up. Finally, the stag fell. Dead. The six of us panting around it.

Sulio was smiling, we all were. It was a fine creature, well hunted. Maccus was the first to smear its blood across his cheeks.

'We must work quickly, before we lose the light,' said Sulio. Without much communication we made a fire and a shelter of sorts. Vannii was in a sulk, perhaps because he had not made the kill. Kennan whistled for Redak, but she did not come.

'It's not like her to wander, not with a kill.'

'Are you sure you kept her back? She may have got kicked.' Maccus had not meant the remark as a criticism but, typical Kennan, he took it that way.

'Of course,' he snapped.

I looked at him, I knew him. He was defensive because he had not kept her back. Now she was missing. He called her again and again. He wandered away.

'Wait, make a torch,' suggested Goliath. 'We'll go and search for her.'

Sulio and I cut branches of green pine with our hand-axes, while Maccus tore strips from the edge of his tunic. Smearing the cloth in pine resin he wrapped it around the end of the sticks. The two torches took a few moments to light, but once they did, we set off to find the hound.

'I'll wait here,' Vannii said, kicking his foot at the dead stag.

We wandered about calling her name, trying to retrace the veering path of the hunt. Faint moonlight gave some light but the flickering torchlight reflected off the undergrowth as we looked for the smooth coat of the dog.

'Over HERE, she's here.' We all ran towards Goliath. 'An ARROW! Look, she's HIT.'

Kennan said nothing, though his hand shook as he bent down to her.

'Wait,' I said. I tried to think of the healing herbs Veryan Hen would use and fumbled in the poor torchlight to find the jagged, kidney-shaped leaves for dressing wounds.

The others went quiet. I looked at them.

They were all looking at me.

My arrow, its white flight feathers, protruded from the dog's side.

24

'I will kill you now,' Kennan spat through his teeth. 'My god, I will kill you now.'

Maccus stepped between us. 'Kennan, it was an accident. Kennan, let's see to Redak, perhaps we can save her.'

'She's DEAD.' He swung Maccus out of the way. I stepped back.

'Come on, Kennan.' Sulio tied to pull him back. 'It was an accident.'

No words formed in my mind. I was as shocked as any of them, but I knew nothing would stop Kennan.

Stepping back, my muscles woke into life. My body prepared for the impact as he launched himself at me. Goliath and Sulio still tried to pull him back but he shook them off. Wrestling in the dark, the undergrowth tugged at my legs. I must not fall. He grabbed me, hatred in his clutches. The others shouted at him to stop. His angry fingers pinched at me as he tried to pull me down. I fought back, but my guilt at killing his dog blunted my edge. I was on the back foot. I was losing.

I was over. On my back. His hands around my throat.

The others pulled him off and I got to my feet. Sulio planted the torch into the ground and tried to reason with Kennan who took out his knife, lashing out at any who would intervene. 'This is my fight,' he shouted to them. 'He tried to kill our father, now he's killed my DOG.'

I wanted to say something but was lost for words.

178

Kennan held his long knife in front of him. I took my axe from my belt. Armed, we circled and side-stepped. Would our feud be resolved here, far away from home, deep in a forest?

I held my axe, two-handed, above my head. Block downward – the way Jay had taught me. He jabbed at me. I brought the axe crashing down. Kennan jabbed again. His blade stung my chest, slitting skin as he swiped it away from my axe blade. First blood to him.

'That's enough now,' Maccus said and repeated. But it continued, several light cuts in my clothes and skin. After a downwards sweep of my axe, I used the momentum and rammed him with the butt end: a rib-cracking blow that took the wind and pace from the fight.

I hesitated, hoping he was finished. But he recovered himself and launched in again before I was ready. His blade gleamed orange in the torchlight and sliced down my arm as I blocked the movement.

Ignoring the fierce stinging of my wounds, the blood dripping down my arm, I raised the axe and I fought on. Twice more I struck him with the back of the axe. Spinning around, I smacked him, first on the thigh, then his side. Severe blows had I used the blade.

Redak's death was an accident. But Kennan's hatred bubbled over beyond reason. A spoilt child who hated to accept he may be wrong. Self-righteous and scornful, he blamed me but he should have kept his dog back in the chase of the hunt. It was his fault, not mine.

There was only one way this would end, with one of us dead. The next swing of the axe must not be the flat or the back, but the sharpened edge of the blade.

He jabbed in once again. I brought my axe down with such a force it knocked the knife from his grip as the shaft impacted his wrist, the blade cutting deep into the earth. He grabbed the torch, still guttering and burning the sticky pine resin.

I tugged at the axe, twisting it to release it from the earth's grip.

Orange light swerved into my eyes.

I screamed. Molten, sticky pine resin, bonded against my melting skin. Searing pain filled me. I choked on smoke and the pungent aroma of burning hair and flesh. Though it was dark, all I could see was a flashing orange, my head was on fire.

The axe forgotten. The fight disregarded.

My hands instinctively covered my smouldering skin.

My fingers burning, my face dissolving under them.

I stumbled away, falling into the damp undergrowth, seeing only orange and black. An instinct for survival drove me to flee. To get away from them all. I crawled on my elbows and dragged my legs. Someone called out for me, searching the ferns. Like an animal, I wanted to hide until my pulse slowed.

The voices behind me, Kennan shouting and ranting as the others restrained him. The cool evening dew sent a blackness to my brain. I blinked, but saw nothing.

**

The woodland was dark. The pain in the side of my head knocked out all reasoning. My natural impulse was to keep moving, my forearms sensing a route through the trees and undergrowth. I was unaware of anything but a motion forwards. Unaware of the foxes, badgers, bats, and dormice that foraged at night, unaware of the sharp scraping plants that left diagonal scratches across my forearms.

I smelt the damp earthy air, my elbows detecting the wetter ground. I crawled towards it. I heard the trickle of water; my mouth was as dry and cracked as baked clay. Thirst propelled me to reach it.

In the cold of the stream, my burned hands stung. I cupped the water into my mouth, spitting out bits of the woodland. Exhausted, my head flopped into the shallow edge, the cold water trickling around my scorched face and ear.

I woke to the sound of birdsong, shivering in the cold surroundings and the memory of suffering. I was alive. I sat myself up and fumbled for the pouch of plant specimens and found the jagged kidney-shaped leaves; for wounds, old Veryan had shown me.

I rubbed them into my hands, spreading their sap into my fingers, and placing more cold wet leaves against the side of my head, binding them in place with a torn strip from my worn out and blood-stained tunic as best I could with shaking hands. I leaned over to drink from the stream, and felt sick immediately afterwards. I needed help.

I stumbled through the forest, falling at times and sleeping where I fell. The day before I walked happily, now the trees were a continual endurance to pass between. And the Jay was coming to the village for me while I was lost in the forest, flesh melted away from my face. I must survive and get back. I ate un-ripened berries, leaves and buds, lichen, grubs and beetles. How many days? Eventually, I approached the thin woodland where the ground-elder grew, not so far from home. I spotted a figure walking my way.

A confident walk, a soft step, a person in tune with the natural world and a gentleness that made both people and animals trust him. Maccus, thank God. Emerging from the trees, I raised my arm before I fell to the ground once again.

'I've been watching for you,' he said as he reached me. 'I searched for you in the forest, but you disappeared. I knew you'd hide, and that you'd return if you could.'

I did not say a word. My voice was as broken as the rest of me.

'You're in a bad way, Luca. Take my arm.' There was strength in Maccus I had not noticed before. The relief of his sure touch on my arm brought tears welling into my eyes. I'll get you back to our place and fetch Veryan Hen.'

**

It was good to be inside. The colours of the fire danced across the roof beams, the smoke and cooking smells lingered, the warmth clung to the walls and the blankets. I fell into a deep sleep at once. When I awoke, I smelled spearmint and rosemary: Veryan Hen.

'You're alive, lad, that's all that counts.' His familiar old voice reassured me like nothing else could. 'You will mend. There is still a future to look forward to.' He indirectly referred to the Jay with a knowing nod of his head. He was impressed with my bandage of leaves. 'St John's wort, we call this plant. Yes, just the thing for burns and wounds, my young friend. Your help to me has given you skills you did not seek but have found...' He gently peeled away the soggy leaves sticking to my face. I gasped at the pain. Bellicia was staring at me. She cried when I raised my head, and ran from the hut.

My teeth clenched hard to stop a scream escaping as the old man washed the burns with cold water. All the while his voice was kind. He told me of worse wounds that he had seen healed. Tales of soldiers and heroes, gruesomely scarred and long remembered.

'St John's wort and myrtle...' He was mixing a new salve for me. 'Rose petals and vinegar wine... Lavender and comfrey...' Bellicia returned, peering around the doorframe. 'Bellicia, fetch your brother, I'll need you both to hold him down.'

They pressed down on my shoulders and legs, their grip hardening as I moved beneath them. The old man's fingers smeared a paste over my cheek and my ear. It was like being burned all over again. I groaned and the air caught in my throat. My open eyes saw only black. Voices sounded distant and muffled. My body moved without my consent. I was falling into a deep, deep cavern.

When I came back to myself, I lay with a thick bandage around my head. Veryan Hen was waiting for me. 'So, lad, you've returned to us. I fear that this may bring on a fever, I'll mix you a drink to try to avert it. You are young and strong, you'll fight it if it comes, I'm sure...

'Your ear is the worst damaged and I can do little about that. It may well be painful as it heals, but will find its own way to improve in time. You'll scab and then scar, but that will show suffering endured and respect demanded. But all in good time.'

His only instructions were, 'don't touch it,' and, 'sleep now.'

**

Sixteen days I lay still, surrounded by the easy family life of Maccus and Bellicia. The world outside bloomed with the early onset of summer, occasional butterflies and bees wafted curiously in and out. I scarcely lifted my head from the blanket. Sticky liquid oozed from the bandage, drying and matting into my hair. Bellicia helped me to eat. Minura sometimes came by, but never for long as Lucanus kept her busy.

My head pounded in the bright sun and I was glad of the shade and the stillness of the days. As my head healed the itching began. I soon learned that to scratch brought a return of the agony for half of the day. Instead, I bit at my fingers or punched at the earth.

In this family I lived amongst, I watched as an observer. There was a calm quiet, an easy cooperation, nothing like the continual tension of my own homelife. Bellicia's mother was always busy yet was never rushed. She always had time to spare for a word of encouragement or kindness, a smile or light touch. There was no argument or raised voice, no bickering or barked demands. The confident peace that radiated from the family touched me and gave me strength.

I was grateful but could do little for them in return and I guessed my presence caused a difficulty for Maccus' father. At the communal wheat sowing, Maccus told me that Lucanus had made a remark to which his father replied, '*He'll shelter under my roof as he heals, but then he'll go his own way.*'

He kept me informed of the other talk in the village. Kennan led many to believe I had deliberately killed his dog. I knew that Vannii and probably Goliath would take his side, of Sulio I was not so certain. Unsurprisingly, Lucanus was quick to believe the fiction, but I was taken aback at how much influence he held. As a man in the Market Traders' Council of Glevum, he was the contact to the wider world, and few would side against him for me. Divisions meant trouble, and the one thing agreed on by all, was that the sooner I left the better.

The Jay had not come. We all waited for news of the battle but none more than me. Finally, word of defeat reached our back-water village. Cynric Claw-hand had won. The hillfort of Sarum was now a strategic post for King Cynric to launch further attacks into the Atrebates lands, and perhaps our own. The disaster lay heavy, as if the air itself contained it. Most knew of someone who had died as the tales of tragedy and failure filtered in. People were quiet, solemn, and morose, the losses affecting us all. Was my father dead?

25

The blossom dropped and the first fruits ripened. I itched for word of my father. Forcing myself to action, commanding my legs and arms to move and to get up, I crossed the threshold and fell over in a heap. Maccus sat me up and dragged me back to lean against the shade of the doorpost. The sun's rays on my legs revived me. 'I will leave soon,' I said.

'Well, not today or tomorrow,' he replied.

Later, Veryan Hen came back. I watched him approach, his bent posture so awkwardly defying nature. He twisted his head in the usual way, calling out his greeting with a smile. His suffering made me bear my own with more grace. He unwound the bandages, while Bellicia stared. She did not cry this time and the cool air on my face was welcome. I felt better than I had for days. 'What does it look like?'

'The torch must have struck you at an angle, scorching your cheek, burning the upper part of your ear, and the hair above,' the old man explained. 'Your young skin is healing well, my friend, though you'll be going nowhere just yet.'

'Is... Has...' He knew what I was trying to ask.

'The battle was lost but *some* escaped. Some have made it homeward.'

I knew what he meant. So, the Jay had survived. 'Wounded?'

'Yes, but will heal, just as you will.'

I took in a deep breath and let it out as a sigh. Relieved he was alive.

I cursed Kennan. The fight and my horrific injuries; I would take the pain but the delay in being with my father was something that brought the taste of hatred into my mouth.

I forced my shoulders to relax. I would not think about Kennan. The war was a distraction. And there was comfort in the presence of my old friend, and the attention of Bellicia. 'Tell me about the battle,' I asked though the tightness of my tongue. 'What have you heard?'

'The Jutes and Saxons combined, were a large force: disciplined, organised, and determined.'

'But what went wrong?'

'We did not have the relics of St Alban,' Bellicia said fiercely. 'We'd have been certain of victory then.'

'The simple truth is that our army was too few and spread too thin. With no prepared strategy they could not make use of the best men or the landscape, instead, were attacked from three sides. Now the great hillfort is lost.'

'If no-one had ever mentioned the relic,' I asked, 'would we've been better prepared?'

'There's no answer to that. It's not worth the worrying.'

'But if we'd had the re—'

'The battle was *not* lost because we didn't have the relic,' old Veryan cut across Bellicia. His face twisted to one side to peer at her, one eyebrow raised, lines deeply furrowed in his forehead. 'But because we were not well prepared.' He turned back to me, tilting my chin to better examine my ear.

Bellicia pressed her lips together. Like many, she believed the relics were our only hope but she would not argue with Veryan Hen.

'Does this hurt?' He pressed against my neck below my ear.

'Not much, though the top of my ear throbs incessantly.'

'Your neck is just bruising. The blisters of your cheek have scabbed and new skin will grow. This ear will take longer.'

'But how long until…'

'Not yet. I'll tell you when. You just mend so you're ready to travel. Yes, the ear will heal in time. The hair above it may never grow back, but the new scars will harden and serve you well enough. The skin is very red but this will fade. Your hearing may be affected… Time will tell.'

'You look like a black grouse from this side,' Bellicia said. 'Dark eyes, red face framed by your black hair.' I smiled, and realised that my scars warped my cheek, already pulling that side of my mouth into a grin.

Bellicia washed my hair and thin pieces of skin flaked away but the new skin beneath thickened quickly, though the itching was unbearable.

Slowly energy returned to me, my appetite too. Once I began to move and to eat, with just a light bandage over my ear, I could make myself useful to my hosts. I sat shelling new beans and grinding corn, mending the broken ox harness, sharpening the plough blade, axes and knives, or stitching leather boots. I watched this family as an outsider, an observer of kindness, patience, and humour. But I longed to be with my own father, in his home, with his family.

**

I regained enough strength to walk around the village, avoiding Kennan or Lucanus. To prove to Veryan Hen I was ready to leave, I walked all the way to the monastery. And I wanted to say farewell to Father Faustus and Crab too.

The walk was slow, stopping often. I arrived to find Crab mending a little cart. As I looked closer, I could see it was a chair, and he was attaching it to an axle and wheels.

'Ahh, for Father Faustus,' I said. Crab smiled and nodded and demonstrated with gestures. I went inside to find the old monk propped up in his bed with a board across him, writing.

'Good day, lad.' He looked at me, considering. 'You look like someone set fire to your head! What can I do for you? You have not come for lessons, or food for the village, I'm guessing.'

'No. I… How are you? Your feet are mending?'

'Not really. I'm too old. My body has given up mending, I think. Though Crab is making me some contraption to *wheel* me about. Did I not say he is a creative genius?'

'Yes, I saw it. It's very good! He looks after you well.'

'When he came to me his mother said he was a burden she could no longer bear. I believe I have given him a chance to thrive where others would not. He has proved himself useful many times over.' He looked back at me, curiously. 'Well, what a pair we make, you and I!'

'I came to say goodbye.'

I told him of my real father and the new future I hoped for. He looked at me sadly and said, 'I hope your heart finds peace where the world cannot, and your wounds heal better than mine.'

I did not want to talk of my wounds or my heart, so I said, 'You are writing? Your Chronicle?'

'Yes, come and see.'

Beneath a list of entries, I watched his quill etch the shiny wet ink into the parchment:

552: In this year Cynric, son of Cerdic, fought at the place called Sarum and put the Britons to flight.

'Tomorrow, your father will come for you,' Veryan Hen whispered. His bent-over posture had worsened over the years and he had to twist his head right up to look at me as we passed on the green.

I barely slept. I was awake at the first light of dawn. My re-stitched deer-hide bag packed and waiting for a new adventure. Bellicia woke too.

'Come with me, I have something for you.'

Without a word I followed her. She led me out past the huts and into the meadow towards the woodland. I leaned on her as we walked through the long grass, campion, and daisies. Buttercups and poppies were reaching up for a place in the early sun, showing their colour and beauty to the waking insects passing by. She sat down in the seclusion of tall stems and bushes pulling me next to her. I moved the other side so my burned face was away from her and she would not have to look at it. She leaned against me with her bare leg nudging against mine.

'Did you ever really like Vannii?' I asked. I did not want to spoil the moment but there were things between us we had to settle. I wondered about Kennan. How much had she encouraged him? I pictured him showing her how to use his bow, the gifts she had not given back. Had she led him on? She liked to be liked. Well, we all do.

'Vannii? I used to. But he's so in love with himself... Luca you're such a fool. I wanted to make you jealous... and I wanted to hurt you like you hurt me.'

'I was hurt. And jealous. But my mother... I'm sorry.' I had no idea what else to say.

'You just can't talk about how you feel, can you? It's no wonder though, with that brute Lucanus for a father – I suppose he's beat talking out of you.'

She was right, I was not used to explaining myself. For so long I had kept my feelings shut from the world as his stick left its mark on my skin. I had told her I was leaving but held back from telling her of the Jay, it was too complicated. So, I slipped my arm around her. She pressed herself against me and breathed out, comfortable and easy.

'Bellicia…' My voice came out a hoarse whisper as her hair tickled my cheek. 'You have something for me?'

'A gift.' She smiled, pushing me back into the long grass. She moved over on top of me. Obscuring the low morning sun, her hair glowed like the halo of an angel. I held her hips as they moved against mine. It was a farewell gift like no other.

When Bellicia and I returned to the hut, Maccus was there.

'Luca, I've been looking for you, where've you been?' He smiled and waved his hand, dismissing the need for an answer. 'There's talk in the village, and this time it's not about you.'

'That's good, the sooner I'm forgotten the better.'

'That spy is back. The red-cloaked man that was seen over the winter? He's here, in the village! He was spotted yesterday and Vannii and Kennan have gone to fetch Aurelius' men.

'Kennan?'

'Yes, he and Vannii went yesterday, they say they'll claim a reward this time.'

'This time?'

'Yes, Luca, you must've known! When they told the soldiers they suspected the monks were concealing the relic? But nothing was found so there was no reward.'

I said nothing. I was taking it all in. My father, the Jay, was in the village. Kennan had gone for the soldiers. Kennan had betrayed Father Faustus.

'But if the soldiers catch the spy,' Maccus was still talking, 'this time they hope for a silver coin.'

My own brother had been the cause of the torture to Father Faustus. That figure sneaking away from Veryan Hen's hut in the night, I had suspected it was Kennan. He overheard our conversation. So, in a way, I was to blame as Father Faustus had believed.

'A silver coin?' My fingers pressed on the coin stitched into the hem of my cloak, the one Aurelius gave me in the market. Kennan had mocked me for it. I realised Maccus was still speaking.

'...Then, at first light he was seen here, right on the edge of the village! Behind old Veryan's hut!'

Kennan had gone to fetch the soldiers. The Jay would be beaten if he were found. 'Yesterday? Vannii and Kennan went yesterday?'

'Yes, Luca, your wits are slow since the burning to your head! They'll be back anytime soon. We could be watching a man-hunt right here in the village.' I looked at Maccus, my gentle friend, caught up and animated with the news gossiped and spread through the village. It was too much to think about all at once, I focussed on the part most pressing and urgent.

'He's no spy.'

I stood up, too quick and wobbled before finding my balance.

'Luca? What do you mean? What do you know?'

'I must find him and warn him.'

**

I ran towards the old man's hut. Villagers were gathering, Kennan and Vannii among them. It was all happening so fast. Hoof beats, and the bobbing heads of six soldiers, gave warning of the hostile approach. I stood on the green, between them and Veryan Hen's hut.

My mind struggled to keep up with events. Their horses rushed by me, the air ruffling my hair and cloak. The drumming hoofs thundered along with my heart. People followed, jostling me as they passed. The riders swung down from their saddles. My feet moved; my head spun. I lurched along with the crowd to the familiar roundhouse where I had spent so many days. Four of the soldiers filed in through the low doorway.

Two figures were dragged out.

One, my old friend who had patched up my wounds, made potions for loved ones, taught me the harp, and told tales of the past – a tiny, frail old man, a hunched over back, and legs that could no longer straighten. The other, a proud and strong warrior. My father. He stumbled on a weakened leg. He held one arm protectively across his chest. Fresh wounds from the battle of Sarum. His lip pinched as if to conceal a wince of pain.

Veryan Hen looked smaller than ever, twisted and thin. He was thrown to the ground. He lay awkward and weak, pinned down by the booted foot of one soldier.

The red cloak was ripped from the Jay. Dark hair and the feathered braids were grabbed by a burly man with a bald head and stubborn jaw.

There was a look of surprise on my father's face. The whites of his eyes and the set of his chin. The men circled and snarled like wolves. Helmets and breastplates, leather leg guards and metal platelets; soldiers ready for a fight with an unarmed and innocent man. Two with clubs, curled lips and tight tendons in their necks, swung blows to his back, his legs, and his head. He crumpled. A wounded fighter with no chance to fight.

'No. No, you are wrong...' Veryan Hen shouted but his voice was lost. He struggled and was stamped on.

'No mercy for spies,' the snarling leader spat out, as his men kicked and battered the Jay, gasping and moaning in the dirt. 'Stay back, everyone, or go back to your business.'

'He's no spy!' I shouted, pushing and shoving through the crowd to reach my father. I grabbed at the leader who swung his fist into the side of my head. The fire of my wounds stunned me, knocking all sound from the world. I fell down.

What began as excitement in the crowd, turned to anger and outrage. The petty gossip of spies was forgotten at the brutal treatment of our benevolent old healer, his guest beaten savagely on the communal green; a place of feasting and cooperation.

Maccus pulled me up. Other villagers pushed forward and tried to intervene, to stop the violence, but were pushed back and threatened themselves.

'No! His name is the Jay, he's a warrior of Powys. He's no Calchwynedd spy!' I yelled out but was pushed back by a thick-set leathery soldier. My arm was twisted behind me as I watched in horror.

Bloodied and broken, the limp figure that had once been a majestic horseman, was hauled up against the door post and held in position by big hairy hands. Through the clamour of the crowd, his eyes met mine. A split-second connection between father and son…

The leader flashed his knife blade and slit the Jay's throat.

26

A gush of red darkened his chest. The high set of his shoulders dropped. His knees buckled and the fine warrior flopped lifeless to the ground. My own blood drained away. My own knees buckled beneath me but hands held me up. Jolting my breath back with a gasp, they turned to Veryan Hen. The cold air of panic choked the breath from me.

'Spies will not be tolerated. Harbourers of spies must be dealt with equally.'

Snapping out of the terror, I wrenched free of the hard grip and surged forward, pushing others out of the way. Forcing myself past Vannii and Kennan, I threw myself between the old man and the lead soldier.

'He was no spy! And this man is no harbourer of spies,' I shouted, desperation overtaking the shock.

'Out of the way, lad.' A huge man grabbed me. I kicked out at his shin.

'You'll not touch him,' I growled. I stood my ground.

Someone stood beside me; Maccus and his mother, pulling his father alongside her. 'This man is old, he's not long for this world, but he's our healer. Without him many in this place and beyond will not see another winter through.'

One or two others stepped up. My eye caught a broad man in the crowd, Lucanus. He did not meet my gaze but also came forwards to protect the old twig of a man who my mother had cared for.

More followed Lucanus.

Hesitation flashed across the soldier's face. He stepped back.

Kennan and Vannii, having brought the soldiers, were in no position to object to the violence, but found themselves in the minority.

The soldiers were halted, reluctant to take on a large group of villagers for an ancient old man so close to death anyway. Shrugging their shoulders, they turned back to the dead man that really mattered, their dirty work still not done. They dragged my father, the Red Horseman, with neither a red cloak nor a horse, to the nearest tree.

Strung up by his feet, he hung for all to see the fate of the enemies of King Aurelius.

**

I tried to carry the old man, but he weighed more than my weakened bones could manage. Helped by others, we got him inside. I gave instructions to settle him in his chair and build up his small fire to make him a brew. Respectfully, I was obeyed.

'Luca will tend to me.' His strained voice reached through pain. 'Leave me now, and go back to your lives.'

Everyone left me to care for the old man, as he had done for me so often before. I forced myself to focus through the shock of what had just happened. 'Where are you hurt?' I asked, examining blood on the side of his head.

'The bones in my hips scream louder than usual, but you'll not fix that. The worst is deep inside; I've lived too long and seen too much. Now the cruelty of life aches within me. Nothing a poultice or bandage will cure.'

Images of the Jay, his body swinging upside down, lifeless and empty, were flashing into my mind. He had haunted my dreams since I first saw him. His embrace had been a brief cloak of happiness and love. He was my hope and future. I clutched at the old man's thin shirt and sobbed into his shoulder.

'That was a bad ending for such a man as he,' the old man wheezed, his gnarled fingers stroking my hair. 'He was a man of principle and honour.'

We stayed still, Veryan Hen and I. The world spun around me, blurring with death, torture and pain for the ones that I loved.

A cramp in my knees made me rise. Pulling a blanket around my wounded old friend I placed a log on his fire. I rifled through his dried leaves: yarrow and a pinch of henbane. Then steeped them in a little clay pot hanging from the fire-dog, adding camomile and sage. He hummed an old tune which he'd taught me on the harp, a lament for death.

I stirred in a little honey, more water, and crushed a small piece of charcoal between fingers and thumb. My cheeks wet as I worked, his cracked old voice murmuring the melody. I hummed along, the soulful notes an echo of despair.

Kennan betrayed Father Faustus for the promise of a silver coin. He brought the murderous soldiers to Veryan Hen's door. Life was cut from the Jay as my brother stood by, watching.

I held the clay cup to the old man's thin lips and he sipped at the brew. The rising steam obscured the tears that ran down the wrinkled grooves of his face. I stayed with him until he fell asleep.

**

Walking away from the old man's hut, I held on to those brief encounters with the Jay over so many years; they were like rare ingots of gold.

He had given me nuts when I was scrawny and thin. We had shared sighting of owls. He had asked me once how old I was; *old enough to do and to go where you choose,* he had said. Might he have offered a place in his home then, if I had simply said *yes?* All that time he had been watching me. His dark eyes – *like a bird of prey*, Bellicia had recently said of mine. I had his black hair and narrow face. He was from Powys in the far western hills, the place of bards and tellers, and had played beautiful music on a lyre; might he have taught me? He had fought at and survived the battle of Sarum and had plans for me.

I stood at the tree where he hung by his ankles. Blood still dripped into the reddening pool beneath. He swung in a slow silent rhythm that was drawn by the air and the world.

My mother had loved him seventeen years ago. I pulled the little jay feathers from his black braids and smoothed the fine filaments together between my fingers: iridescent black and blue stripes. I had made a jay for my mother when first allowed in the pottery, she kept it until the clay dried and crumbled to dust. I pictured her wiping her cheek as she swept it up and threw the remnants outside. She had still loved him.

A figured stepped from the shadows: Bellicia. She turned and I followed her back to the meadow. As we sat, she took the feathers from my hand. 'You knew him then.'

'Yes. He was a warrior of Powys, just returned from Sarum, where he fought for us all.' I could not tell her he was my father. That required an explanation I was too emotional to give.

She pulled a loose thread from the edge of her shawl and began to braid the feathers into my hair. 'Keep still.' Her whisper against my cheek brought tears that slid down and dropped from my tightened jaw. 'You will still leave?'

Hope of a future with Aurelius was over. I could not serve the king now. But I might go to the far western hills; someone should tell them of the Jay's death. Who better than I? If I looked as like him as Veryan Hen suggested, I may be accepted. I had not forgotten the other revelation, my own existence was bound with Ceawlin, the Gewisse prince who was prophesised to be *Bretwalda*.

Was my destiny tied to his as the old man had hinted at?

'Yes, I cannot stay here. But first I must look to Veryan Hen. He has suffered too much.'

News of the spy's murder travelled fast, like dandelion seeds on the breeze, from meadow to meadow, until it reached the ears of Cadrawd of the Calchwynedd, rekindling his interest in the place. Defeat had done nothing to lessen the obsession for the relics. I was about to leave the village a second time, when shouts that the monastery was ablaze echoed around the village.

A plume of black smoke rose from that direction. The sensation of blood rushing inside me jolted every muscle to move. I was running.

My pulse was loud in my head. My damaged face tingled as the blood reached its surface. I stumbled, stopping to recover myself. Then followed the path so familiar and filled with good memories. I reached the flint wall.

The smell of burning thatch, old wood, and things that should not burn filled my nose as I coughed my way along it. Heat and smoke swirled around and pricked at my eyes. The large wooden door was broken and swinging diagonally on one hinge. There was no-one to greet me.

I peered through the smoke. The timber huts surrounding the old stone temple were wrecked, partly demolished, partly burned. The temple walls still stood but the roof and the timber chambers behind were a ruin of black smouldering stumps and debris.

The books and parchments from the ancient past were reduced to downward drifting ash. The collection from Glevum entrusted to the monks, the handed-down writings of wiser men, the delicate fragments of knowledge stored, treasured, and learned from over so many years, destroyed. A permanent loss, not burnt skin that re-grows, but more like a heart cut out.

A figure reached me from the smoky ruins, one shoulder higher than the other. Crab.

Soot dirtied and tear-streaked, he pulled at my arm, leading me into the temple. 'No, Crab. It's too dangerous.' The new scars on my head burned in memory, preventing me from entering. Charred roof beams clung above, some falling around us.

But Crab whimpered and tugged and yanked me inside. In the centre of the temple, surrounded by shimmering heat, smouldering, smoking remains, he pointed to the floor. The mosaic of Venus, the bare-breasted beauty I had looked at so often.

'What? What is it?' I was baffled. Crab cried and pointed, but I did not understand; I did not want to be there. 'We must go. Come on, come away, Crab.'

He held my arm in a painful grip, nearly pulling me over as he kicked awkwardly at the debris at the edge of the pattern, pointing again. I saw it.

'What's that?' The pattern disguised a groove in the floor. 'Is it a hatch, a trap-door?'

He nodded and brushed the ash away with his foot. As more of the edge was exposed, I began to help him. A roof beam crashed behind us. My instinct was to leave, but I knew whatever was beneath this floor mattered to Crab.

I knew what it was.

I could not leave it either.

'Hurry, help me move this timber.' We worked together clearing the fallen roof tiles and beams as fast as we could until three sides of the hatch could be seen. Prising my fingers into the groove, I lifted the lid. Crab helped me heave open the secret hatch.

A new cloud of smoke billowed up from the hole. I could see

nothing at first. Then the bald top of a head.

Father Faustus.

With a last shove of the hatch, crashing over and smashing pieces of mosaic into the sooty remains, I reached down to my old teacher.

He was dead.

Not burned. The smoke and heat must have overwhelmed him in the small hole. I tried to pull him up but there was no way we could lift him. Crab sniffed and sobbed, but was pulling at a hemp sack the old man clutched. 'Leave him, Crab. We can do nothing for him now.'

But the mute lad persisted, so I helped. Prising the stiffened fingers away from the sacking we pulled it free. I looked inside.

The gleam of gold, the flash of green gems, the casket that had been searched for with violence and death.

I looked away, closing the sack, fearing for my life.

I offered it back to Crab. He would not touch it. Shaking his head and waving his hands, he kept indicating to me. I should have it. I should take it.

Then he pulled at a cord around his neck, a small key dangled. A tiny silver gleam in the gloom of the smoking ruins. Snatching it free, he gave it to me.

I took it.

27

I ran. My pulse pounded in time with my feet. I looked about, fearful. I must get off the path. I threw myself amongst the tall thin stems of cow-parsley. Barely breathing, I waited for any sign I had been followed or that anyone else was about.

Did the box contain the relic of St. Alban? Carefully drawing the casket into the opening of the sack, I slipped the key into place. It clicked as it released. I opened the lid, running my fingers over the smoothed gold edges. Inside was a dirty fragment of cloth. I dared not look. But I needed to know. I lifted out the cloth, unrolling the stiff fabric, fearful it may disintegrate. There was no weight in it, but the rough dusty texture seemed to imprint itself into my hand.

Tiny brown finger bones lay end to end, on a dark smear the shape of a finger. St Alban's finger, wrapped in a torn edge of his blood-soaked tunic.

Everything went silent and the world spun about me. Was it the presence of God? Had I just cursed myself for the unworthy sinner I was? I quickly re-rolled the bones and put them back in the gold casket, locking it and pushing it into the sack.

I cried. Father Faustus, that clever man would no longer pass on his knowledge. The world had lost something special. He had taught other boys, perhaps through them something good would come. The monastery was gone, the books and future learning gone with it. All the old monk's work. What would become of Crab?

So much was lost. My whole body wracked with the pain of it.

Eventually I took the path home, but I could not take the sack into the village. I veered off into the wood, to a place avoided by all – the Bear's Cavern. I dropped down into the cold and hid the sack that contained the precious gold casket, and within that, the powerful finger bones of the saint. I had grown taller since the night Kennan left me in there, though it was still difficult I managed to climb back out.

In the village, I came face to face with Lucanus. We stared at each other, neither friendly nor hostile. There was too much between us to be as simple as that.

'The monastery?' he asked.

'Burned to the ground. Father Faustus is... gone from this life, he is with God.'

I detected sympathy in his look before he turned away. I stumbled into Veryan Hen's hut. The old man was dozing on his sheep hide. I pulled the thick felt blanket over him and tucked the end under his head. Then slumped down myself and entered a deep and disturbing sleep.

When I awoke, the birdsong rang out with the new day. Veryan Hen was still, his hand hanging limply. I took it in mine to tuck it under the blanket, stone cold.

He too was dead.

**

All in the village mourned Veryan Hen. He had touched every life in Framlutum. Bound in a wool shroud, he was carried out by six men, though two would have easily managed. The small bent figure was a vast wealth of wisdom. His loss left me empty of everything but anger.

Kennan.

Cadrawd may never have come back to search the monastery if Kennan had not betrayed Father Faustus in the first place, or fetched the soldiers for the Jay. He had brought death to the three men that mattered to me. Each had given me hope and the possibility of a future, and all had died as a consequence of *his* actions.

I saw him in the crowd, hair loose and shoulders relaxed. Hatred drove every weakened muscle to action. I crossed over the green in a few paces, scattering others and swung my clenched fist hard into his face. The impact jolted my shoulder and my knuckles clicked painfully.

'It's not my fault he died.' He spat red. 'Don't take it out on me.' His voice cracked as he pressed his bleeding nose. 'He'd have died soon anyway, he was old…'

I burned with fierce need to hurt him, to damage his face as he had mine. To take the breath from his mouth, to spill his blood. I side kicked his knee, his weakness, and looked around for a weapon.

Then his fist met my ribcage. I sunk to my knees.

'Luca, will you never stop? Can't you tell when you're beaten?'

I forced myself up to face him. 'I'm not beaten.'

'Look at yourself. You're weak and useless. You should have died in the forest—'

I lunged at him to scratch out his eyes, but hands held me back. Irritated villagers fed up with our feuding. Kennan raised his arm as Lucanus came behind him and dragged him back. 'This village has had enough of your squabbles!'

I was held firm. Lucanus stared at me. 'Luca.' He paused, searching for words that never came easily for him. 'You're cursed and you're damned. Trouble surrounds you. You bring heartache to all…'

'It's time for you to go now, lad,' said another voice. Others joined in muttered agreement. The moment had come, they wanted me gone. The muttering became a sort of chant, the only word I heard was, 'go.'

Go. That word on a breath, sucked my fury from me. The energy I had found from my anger had gone.

205

My shoulders slumped and the hands that held me released their hard grip. Weary and defeated, I staggered to balance myself. I looked at the faces around me, Maccus' father, Maccus and Sulio, and the man whose child I had saved in the flood. They said nothing.

The village survived on cooperation and harmony; I brought out divisions and differences. I must leave. I wanted to leave, but not this way, not as an outcast, not thrown out in a public show of rejection.

A slim wisp slipped out from the crowd, Minura. She embraced me and cried. Maccus stepped forward and drew her back, catching my eye as his arm enfolded her. 'Bellicia, run and fetch Luca's bag,' he called to his sister, knowing she would take the care to pack the essentials for me. 'And his cloak.'

I looked down at myself. I had nothing but the ragged clothes I stood in; my future less certain than ever before.

Step by painful step, I straightened my back and held my head high. As I reached the trackway on the edge of the last hut, Bellicia, Maccus, and Minura came up behind me.

I held my sweet sister for the last time. She had strength under her small frame, so much like our mother. I must let her go.

'It is best, Luca.' Maccus took Min by the hand and gave me my bag, the one I had stitched and repaired a lifetime ago. 'Too much has happened here, you need to find a new path.' He squeezed my shoulder in friendship. 'Farewell and safe travels, my friend.'

Bellicia drew the cloak about my shoulders. That physical touch, light but full of care, made me want to weep. 'I'll be taking a wash down at the pool at first light,' she whispered in my good ear before turning away.

**

I headed for the Bear's Cavern. I had spent a cold autumn night there when I was twelve and was not concerned to be spending another. The place was a sanctuary now.

The tall woodland canopy was thick with the new season's leaves, letting little light reach past the narrow entrance to the cavern. The cool air hit my legs as I dropped down into the darkness. I leaned back, taking in the smell of damp ancient soil, the prickling cold a welcome sensation.

I fumbled and reached for the sack containing the casket and relic. For a sickening moment I thought it was gone, then in nauseous relief I brushed the coarse weave of the sackcloth.

I saw the face of the Jay in the rocky edges, Father Faustus' loose robe in the trailing mosses, and Veryan Hen bent over and twisted in the gnarled roots. All dead because of Kennan.

But also because of the relic.

The remains of a dead saint were supposed to ensure divine protection and deliverance from the heathens, but instead had driven men mad for most of my life. Father Faustus had blamed our failure and losses on the sinful ways of our leaders. That pious and devout upholder of God's laws had shielded the relic from becoming the *plaything of kings* – but it had not protected him. He had held it in his hands as he died.

The Jay, a warrior who said he would destroy the relics, went to the battle at Sarum and survived. Veryan Hen had shown me the enemies that threatened us were not devils to be defeated by God, but people with grudges to bear, individuals with their own stories and reasons to hate.

The finger of St Alban had brought trouble, division, and distraction. The Jutes and Saxons were united and stronger than ever, the Atrebates were a broken people, while the Dobunni and the Calchwynedd were locked in futile competition.

I had seen and touched the old finger bones myself but what had it brought me? Lucanus said I was cursed and doomed, perhaps it is the relic that's cursed. I once dreamed of being the hero that found the old bones but now that possession was an unwelcome burden.

What should I do with them?

Destroy them as my father would?

Veryan Hen had taught me to question. 'Not all we are told is the truth,' he had said. But truth was out of reach. I needed things beyond doubt.

The stone flecks in the mud walls, the diagonal strips of pallid moonlight cross the entrance hole, the damp moss, and the sounds of small creatures – the things of the earth, were the only things I was certain of.

The whisper of suspicions and assumptions had marred the facts and distorted the history, but the earth cares nothing for that, or for sickness and hunger, droughts and floods. What matters to the earth is worms and beetles, plants and fungi, the rivers and woodland. My trust would be on the things I could see, touch, and smell: the earth, the rocks and the sky. The relic was just the finger bones of a man long dead, and could not hold the fate of Britannia. I would destroy it as my father would have.

But first I would go to the pool to say a proper goodbye to Bellicia.

28

Bellicia sat naked on a mossy rock, hair wet and skin pink, her back to me. I watched her pull her gown over her head, lifting her hair out and squeezing the ends. She looked up as I climbed down.

'I'm sorry you have to leave this way.' Her voice was even and calm. Her lashes black around her blue eyes, intense from her cold morning wash. 'Most see your fight with Kennan as more of your childhood resentments, though we all know you've taken Veryan Hen's death hard.' She stood up, her gown dropping into place as she did. 'But... I *know* there is more.' She looked right at me, challenging, suddenly bitter. 'I know you. But you'll never tell me, you'll never confide in me. I'm just a girl, what would I know?'

I wanted to tell her. I should have told her before. Now it was too heavy and complicated to even begin. I said nothing, giving her little option but to continue.

'Well anyway, you and Kennan are not the only ones to fight, news came in after you left...'

'What news?'

'Aurelius sent men to attack the Calchwynedd. He said, Cadrawd's men had to be punished for what they did to the monastery... But the Dobunni were still weary from the battle. Many are dead.'

'So, the tribes of Britannia kill each other over the dammed relic!' It made me sick.

'You shouldn't speak of St Alban's relic that way,' she chided, surprised at me.

'King Cynric Claw-hand must be sneering at the folly of it all. And what of Aurelius now?'

'I know you intend to serve him but, well… my father says there are challenges to his leadership. He's weak, old, sick, they say he'll not live much longer. Apparently, he cannot choose which of his three grandsons will be fit to rule.'

'I hope it's Prince Coinmail.'

'Father says, Aurelius wants the kingdom divided between them. Things are changing, Luca, you must be careful in Glevum, perhaps you should not go alone.'

'I met Prince Coinmail once…' I said, missing the intent of her last words. 'I liked him. Maybe I will serve him one day.'

'So, you will go to Glevum then?'

I shrugged. 'Maybe, not yet…' The relic had taken over my destiny.

'Luca, how can I make it plainer to you? I will come with you, just ask me!' She stepped up to me. 'I'll leave with you *now*. We can make a new life together. You can trust me, just talk to me. Include me in your mysterious world.'

She stood so close I groaned aloud and shifted away from her.

'No, Bellicia. There's something I must do…'

'Don't shut me out, Luca.' She reached for my arm but I knocked hers away. Her shoulders slumped, rejected. Her gaze dropped.

'What's that?' She pointed at my hand. 'What's that sack?' I shifted it behind me. She knew I had left with only my deer-hide bag and cloak.

'It's nothing—'

'Show me!' She tried to grab it. 'What is it?'

I swung it away from her grasp. 'Nothing.'

'Luca, what are you up to?' Her rejection changed to suspicion.

I should have known that I could not keep such a thing from her. I pushed her back as she reached again.

'Lucanus was right, you're nothing but trouble.'

'Bell, I'm sorry, listen...' I should have just turned and run, but I could not leave it that way. She reached for the sack again. 'STOP, Bellicia.' I held the sack above my head, out of her reach. 'I *can't* tell you. You're right, there *is* more to all this. But there's something I must do... alone...'

With her hand on her hip, defiant and alluring, she looked just as she had when I first noticed how pretty she was. Momentarily unguarded, I lowered the sack.

She grabbed it. It swung back, hitting the rock behind her. It clunked with the ringing echo of metal. We both froze.

'Give it back...'

Her quick mind turning, she looked at me. Then she looked inside, peering at the gold casket.

'Where have you got this?' Her voice breathy and bewildered.

'There's no time to explain.' I snatched it back and she let it go without resistance. I retreated, pacing backwards, my heart thumping right up into my throat.

'But, Luca...'

I began to climb the slope from the pool.

'But *Luca*...' Her voice getting louder.

'Just forget about it,' I shouted down to her. I should have said I would always think of her, I loved her. Life had not been kind and she could not come with me, but she would stay in my memories forever.

'LUCA, you must give it to *Aurelius*... That's where you're going?'

I said nothing. She stared at me.

'You're going to give it to Aurelius, aren't you?'

I could not tell her. I could not lie to her. I said nothing.

'Luca, it could save us. LUCA?'

'No.' Shaking my head, I backed up the slope to the top. 'No.'

'Luca, you must!'

'I *know* what I must do.'

That is the last thing I said.

I left my fate in her hands.

29

Bellicia would tell that I had the relic. How could she not? The desperate hope in them would override any shred of loyalty she had left for me; I had not trusted her. I had rejected her. The hunt for me would soon begin. Kennan would relish the chance to both kill me and return with the longed-for relic.

I must be clever. I must use my wits. But as my feet pounded the soft earth on the familiar track from the village a new weakness shook in my knees. I ignored it and ran. Gain distance, was all I could think. One foot in front of the other, a steady pace so I would not tire.

I was heading back towards the still smouldering monastery. I must skirt around it. Head for high ground, the distant hills. East, towards the rising sun. My pursuers would be looking into the brightness.

I crossed through woods and grassland, streams and scrubland, the hill gently rising, until I reached the steep winding pathway. By then, the sun was already overhead, the hot air above matching the heat seeping up from the ground. As I climbed the hill, I paused to wipe the beading sweat from my hairline. Looking back, small dark shapes were blurring in the distant grassland below: animals grazing or people hunting?

The track grew steeper but tree roots gave me footholds and their canopy gave shelter from sun and from sight. At last, I reached the high ground and woodland stretched out before me. Surely, they would not find me.

But Kennan was an excellent hunter. He could track and kill. He was a good shot with his bow. His arrows had metal tips lovingly filed to a keen point, the shafts scraped smooth and straight, the feathers trimmed to streamlined angles and laced lightly with gut.

I kept going east as the sun ranged westward. Fool, I should have changed direction. I turned south. Trees, hills, streams and crisscrossing paths; I began to zigzag, to dip and to rise; impossible to see behind me, impossible to know if I was followed. Maybe I wasn't, maybe there was no-one there after all. I began to relax, to slow, and even to stop for water. I was hungry. It was a long time since I had eaten, not since I left the village, my belly too twisted and tight.

I had packed my bag in time of happiness and optimism, waiting for the Jay. I opened it to check the wire snare and knife were still there and found three cloth wraps of food; Bellicia. She had given me beans, a lump of smoked fish, and a chunk of rye bread. Now, I had driven her to hate me. All for these cursed finger bones that I carried over hill and dale. The sooner I was rid of them the better, but that was easier to think than to do.

I ate the fish and drank from a stream before moving on again. Somewhere nearby was an abandoned hillfort. High ground must be safer and without a better plan, I instinctively headed for it. The shadows lengthened eastwards in the afternoon sun. My calves tightened from the upwards climbing, sweat ran down my back and my hand ached from clutching the sack. Crossing dry grassland on a high ridge I could see the hillfort ahead.

Men. Many men. I stopped dead.

Trails of smoke, sounds of chopping and raised voices, wafted in the hot breeze. Soldiers were repairing the palisade and ditches, the gates, and the watch tower. I retreated back the way I had come with a sensation of panic in every muscle. I quickly reached the woodland I had zigzagged through, and heard a voice.

I stopped dead once again. The unmistakable voice of Vannii, just a spear's throw from me. I darted sideways. There were other shouts, Goliath and Kennan for sure. Doves scattered noisily upwards, alerting them to my presence. Branches snapped and cracked, revealing my escape. The cursed sack in my grip burned into my palm, the soles of my boots burned into my feet. The rushing sound of my pursuers was right at my back. I dared not look round. My legs fled as my mind tried to think.

I skidded to a stop at a cliff edge before me.

'LUCA!'

Goliath right behind me.

'He's HERE!'

His hand reached out to grab me as I plunged downwards.

Dropping, I hit loose scree. Sliding and skimming, I tried to slow my descent, leaning back into the hill, small stones scraping into my backside. The gold casket was under my hand. The thin fabric of the sack between it and the rocks. The hard shape vibrated, taking the impact of my sliding over the stones, saving my left hand from certain shredding. I heard a howl of someone following behind. Another drop loomed ahead.

A jagged rock stuck out to my right. My smarting fingers grasped it and I swung myself off the scree – just as Goliath slid past me and over the drop.

His scream came to an abrupt end below.

Clambering into the rocks, I scurried down. No time to think about the fate of an old friend turned enemy. I must concentrate on every foot and handhold as I climbed over a precipice. The dust and dried blood on my hands loosened my grip. I spat on them and chanced to look up. Two figures were climbing down the rocks from the top, Kennan and Vannii. But Sulio was now on the rocks, as I was.

A shower of stones skimmed past me. Small ones hit my shoulder and back, painful and sharp.

'Kennan, stop!' Sulio cried out as he was hit too. 'I'm close.' Sulio's voice echoed off the hard rock face. 'I'll get him. Stop throwing stones.'

He was close. Too close.

The sack was making it difficult to climb. Each time I reached for a new hold I nearly fell.

'Luca,' Sulio called. 'Give me that sack. You'll die if you don't.'

'Will you kill me then?' We could not see each other's faces, just the presence of each other and the scuffing sounds of our clambering.

'We just want the relic. Give it to me and I'll let you go.'

A broad grassy ledge was tantalisingly near, just to the right and a bit lower. I took a wide step, too wide and my hand slipped. I launched myself sideways to direct my fall and landed on the ledge, but my legs dangled over. The gold casket hit the rock with a clunk. I was winded. Wriggling myself up, Sulio appeared above me.

He dropped onto the ledge. We both stood still, eyes locked.

'Luca, why are you doing this? Just give me the sack.'

I backed right to the edge. I looked down; more rocks a long way below. There was a tremor in my knees. Should I just give him the sack? I did think about it.

I turned and dropped down once again. Sulio followed, right on my tail. So close. His foot on my fingers. As fast as I could go, he remained right behind. As the ground neared, I took a desperate jump, rolling as I landed, and smacking myself with the gold casket. Sulio landed beside me, grabbing for me as I got to my feet. My heel slipped through his fist.

I ran. He chased.

He was always faster than me. I headed for the trees.

My cloak held me back as he grabbed it.

'Luca, STOP. Damn you. Just give me the sack.'

I stumbled and we both fell. His weight on my legs.

'I can't. You don't understand. There are things I cannot explain.' We looked each other in the eye, both searching for clarity, friendship and reason. 'Sulio, I know it sounds like madness, but there are things you don't know... Trust me, Sulio.'

'You always know more than anyone else, you're always so sure that you're right.'

'Just trust me, Sulio. Please.'

His grip on me still held, but his look suggested the old reluctance to argue. 'So many times, you understood things better than any of us, but this is madness. This is the Relic of St Alban!'

'Just think for a minute. You were always the one to think clearly, you question things like I do. The bones are cursed. Father Faustus protected them but they did not protect him. Think of it, the search has brought trouble and death. That's *why* they've been hidden all this time.' His weight relaxed slightly against my legs. His eyes flicked as they looked into mine. 'What good has this damn relic brought *me*? It's *cursed*.'

Holding my gaze for a moment, he let go of my cloak but still pinned down my legs. 'You've always challenged everything. I liked that about you. But, well... this is too big for either of us.'

'Sulio, Father Faustus knew more than both of us ever will. Veryan Hen knew things of the past. Both older and wiser men understood the relics were *not* best served in Aurelius' hands. The king is mad and the relics are a danger to us all. They've already brought death to so many.'

'Looking back, you've been right more often than not.' He slumped, resigned. 'Luca, I don't understand, but I... I always looked up to you. I *do* trust you.'

He shifted and rolled off me. His hands over his face. 'I just hope you know what you're doing.'

**

I ran, heading westwards, keeping my pursuers facing the lowering sun. In a roundabout way I would keep heading west, towards the land of my father, but first I must somehow shake off my pursuers and destroy the relic.

Of my four hunters only two remained. Vannii and Kennan. The day cooled; I slowed down. I was used to running, but the exhaustion of being chased was draining me. How many more would come after me? No, Kennan and Vannii would have ensured secrecy, wanting to return with the relic as heroes themselves. My doubts also pursued me.

Should I really destroy them? I could not give them to Aurelius, and to give them to Cadrawd would be a betrayal. Though, if they belonged anywhere, it was St Alban, to be returned to the rest of his remains. But then Cadrawd would have won.

No. I must destroy them. I could not burn them as fire would give me away. As I ranged about, I hoped an opportunity might soon present itself. Grassland led on to heather scrub, then through hazel trees and swampy rushes. A small trickling stream wound its way through an oak wood, I stopped and drank. I sat down and ate the bread. It made me hungrier. I wandered on, mushrooms raised their heads and lured me. I was about to pick them, but they were Death Caps. Instead, I ate rowan berries, sharp and tangy, making me feel sick. I kept going, one foot in front of the other – just as my hunters were doing.

The landscape was a friend in my loneliness. Hawthorn and ferns, poppies and campion, falcons and doves, field mice and grass snakes; no complication of people. When we hunted the boar so long ago, we had followed the random trail of a creature with no purpose or place to be. That's how I felt and the wandering suited me.

The sun sunk low in a reddening sky. Would they hunt all night? Surely, they could not track me once the daylight had gone? Perhaps

I should stop, set a trap overnight. I needed meat. A bird or small mammal would do, though I must eat it raw. My stomach growled.

**

I woke, unaware that I had fallen asleep. The early light was lifting with birdsong and dew. I was nestled under a gorse bush I did not remember, and wriggled myself free; my back damp and my hips stiff. My snare was still in the bag waiting for use. Idiot. Where were my hunters? I should not have slept.

I moved on, my hips loosening with every step. I smelt the salt of the great river as ragged bushes gave way to open grassland. A lazy herd of cattle slumbered in the early sun, tails flicking and heads lifting as I passed them.

Soon the ground became soft under foot and grass turned to reed; I was in a swamp. A fat frog jumped across my path. My hunger-honed instinct, swift and sure, caught it by one leg. I smacked its head on a stone, slit the belly and pulled the tiny guts out, nibbling the flesh from the small bones. It tasted of wet earth and oil.

Reaching the great wide river, the high tide gleamed bright. I could throw the casket in, but it must be out in the middle or risk being revealed at low water. The muddy edges emerged as the tide receded. As it ebbed away it left a naked expanse of scattered stones, weed, and wood, all picked at by birds.

This echoed my life: the tide had gone out, leaving my struggle and weaknesses exposed, revealing how little I truly had now the people I cared for were gone. Perhaps, when it flowed back in, gliding over and covering my dirty tracks, it might bring something new.

Trudging along the sandy edge of the bank, I saw a boat. I could cross the river and drop the cursed relic into the middle, leaving my hunters behind. But a man appeared as I approached, his scraggy beard attempted to hide weathered features, his small eyes told of a ruthless suspicion, his gnarly fingers suggested possessions prised from their owners in payment.

'How much to cross the river, good man?'

He looked me up and down, weighing me in his mind. He stared at the sack and then back at me. 'What do you have?'

'Nothing to eat, if that's what you mean.'

'Trinkets or utensils might be considered.' He was looking at the sack. 'A coin would do it, if not.'

My silver coin was still stitched into my cloak. Was that coin for this moment? Was this destiny? The coin that Aurelius himself had given me, to use for the dirty deed of destroying the relic he lived only to find. I looked around as I considered it. And saw a single figure treading the path I had just walked. Kennan.

30

'I have a coin, if you can take me *right now.*' I scratched at the stitching to release my silver as the man craned his head to see it. The ferryman licked his dry lips, wispy eyebrows arching in surprise. 'Right away, young master,' he said with a black-toothed grin.

A pair of sandpipers skipped aside as we pushed the boat into the water. My shoulder to the sternpost, water up to my knees and lapping at the ash planks, the old man boarded the craft in a well-practised step, reaching out to take the sack from me. I ignored him and awkwardly heaved myself over the gunwale as we drifted out. Standing, he used an oar to push us into the mid-stream, then sat down and began to row. The early sun glinted as the little boat bobbed gently over lilting waters. I chanced a look behind. Kennan was on the shore, running to the point I had left.

We were in the mid-stream, the deep-water. The current tugged our little craft seaward and the ferryman added extra pulls to the downstream oar. All I had to do was drop the sack over the side, but it had become stuck in my unloosened grip. Held so long it was part of me, the hope of the Dobunni in my hand. I just could not do it.

The man paused his rowing, eyeing my agitation, eyeing the sack.

'Something wrong, lad?'

I shook my head, hiding my sinking frustration.

He began rowing again, pulling harder to cross the strong centre current. We reached the shallow slack waters nearer the shore. My opportunity missed. I would not fail again.

'Jump out here, it's shallow enough… There's another who waits to cross. See.' He pointed. I could see the small figure of Kennan standing on the shore we had left, watching us. I jumped out, the cold water just over my knees, and waded up the stony bank.

How would Kennan pay to cross? Did he get his coin for the murder of the Jay?

**

I remained close by the shore, trudging north. The bones inside the fragment of cloth, inside the golden casket, inside the sack, held me to the riverside like a magnet. My intention of throwing it in still lurked. The possibility of putting it forever out of reach, kept my feet tracing the edge of the great river, step after step. But the waters were receding.

Ahead, the river stretched around a huge bend. Wet mud gleamed in the morning sun, a vast brown plateau lined by black weeds and pecked at by curlews and dunlins. I crouched on my haunches, skimming stones to bounce over the mud to the weed line and into the falling tide beyond. One patch shone brighter, wetter, softer. I threw in a stone and it sunk with a plop. A soup spot.

Delicate bird footprints decorated the mud, but none near the bright patch, it was left well alone. I found a big stone and stepped carefully forwards, as near as I dared: four footsteps. I heaved in the stone. Landing with a wet splat, I watched as it slowly submerged, its dry tip closing over with liquid mud.

I sat back on the shore, and pulled the casket from the sack, seeing it in the daylight for the first time. The gold was scuffed and dented from fleeing my hunters. Snatching the key from around my neck, I unlocked it for the second time. To be sure. I took out the stiffened roll of dirty cloth and carefully unwrapped the finger. I held the tiny bones my palm.

Hidden all these years, how long had Father Faustus been protecting it? Had someone before him also deliberately concealed it? Maybe someone like me, years before, witnessing the damage it brought. I could hold the bones no longer and was placing them back in the casket when I heard a crunch on the gravel.

I turned. Kennan stood, bow raised, arrow nocked, aimed at me.

I flipped the lid shut, clicked the key. I stood up and faced him.

'Why do *you* have the gold casket, the relic?' He was breathless. 'What do you intend to do with it?'

I said nothing, but took two steps onto the mud, placing my feet in my own prints from earlier. He stepped closer, arrow still aimed at me.

'What are you doing, Luca?' His finger twitched against the taught bowstring, but he did not release it. He was uncertain.

I took two more steps. I looked at him, and threw the casket into the soup spot.

We both watched as it sunk. Brown sludge crept over the gold and green jewels.

It was gone.

'Luca, are you MAD! What have you done?' He lowered his bow, staring into the bright wet patch where the golden casket had been. Throwing down the bow, he raced towards it. I retreated to the gravel.

He started to sink, reaching in, feeling for it, and sinking faster; thigh right in. He tried to turn, to get back to firmer ground, but his foot was sucked in and he fell.

He struggled, but managed to raise himself up, mud coating his side.

'Luca, why? Help me get it out. LUCA!'

The shock of it distracted him from everything else, forgetting that he was going to kill me. Suddenly I was just Luca, his brother.

My throat was dry, my fists by my side. 'The relic is CURSED,' I shouted. Saying it aloud made it feel right. 'It's brought death and disaster, there's a reason it was hidden.'

'Why is it you, Luca? You think you know more than anyone else. Now you think you know better than *God!* Who are you to judge the fate of the relic of St Alban? The devil has cursed you. It's you who've bought death and disaster.'

Shifting his other leg to stand, it began to sink too.

'And yet I had the relic, the precious bones of the martyr…' The words slid out through my clenched teeth. 'Have they brought me peace? Have they brought me divine intervention and saved me from my enemies?'

He stopped moving. He blinked, staring at me. Taking in the words and trying to make sense of them. And then in true Kennan style, when faced with something he could not understand, he lashed out.

'I should've shot you while I had the chance.'

He angrily attacked the mud that held him. He fell again. He sank further. Grunting and huffing as he struggled, his movements the only sounds as he clawed for the firmer mud to pull himself out, but it was too soft.

'Kennan, what happened to the others?'

He looked up, mud was packed into his hair. 'Do you really want to know, do you care?' Mud flicked up across his arm as he tried to raise a leg.

'Yes, I care, tell me. Goliath? Vannii?'

'Goliath was in a bad way, Sulio went back for help. Vannii…' He let out a sigh which turned to a growl. 'Those mushrooms you once told us were poison? Well, he ate some.'

The Death Cap, I had seen them myself, nearly picked one.

'We were hungry… not eaten all day… I left him, sick and breathless.' He struggled further. 'No doubt it will have passed and

224

he'll have gone home.'

'Death Cap, he'll be dead by now.'

He stopped moving and looked at me. I held his gaze, looking into his eyes. I found hatred, undisguised and powerful, that reflected my own.

31

A.D.552

THE BANKS OF THE RIVER SABRINA

So, my brother is up to chest in the soft silt. The sun has followed its path overhead as I've re-lived the events of our lives from the very beginning, now I must decide. For the sake of our mother, should I save him? Or should I indulge my hatred and let him die?

The river, a silver snake lurking low in these mud flats, has grown slowly wider over the day. The dull mud banks that bend to my right are smooth, awaiting their saltwater blanket. The mud around Kennan is churned and scoured by his raking, grasping arms. His contorting efforts to reach firmer mud, to draw himself out of the sinkhole, have left him weary and caked to his chin in mud. He is watching me watching him.

'Why are you still here?'

'I'm thinking.'

'What's there to think about? If I were you, I'd get going, because if I get out of this, I'll hunt you down and not stop 'til you're dead.'

I smile the distorted half grin my scarred face will allow. In my shoes he'd not hesitate to leave me to die. There is heat beneath my scars, smiling does that to me now. Even after so long in the mud, he hates to admit his fate lies in my hands.

'You're an arrogant arse, Luca. You think you're above God. You'll burn in hell after today.'

'And what of you? When you pass from this life into the next you will need a silver coin to pay the ferryman. I hope you still have yours, you earned it. You thought only of the reward and claiming to be the hero. That's why you have followed me here, isn't it? So you can be the hero with the relics? Yet how many have died?'

'I never meant the soldiers to hurt Veryan Hen. You cannot hold that against me.' Though his face is splattered in mud, I see he is frowning. 'I liked the old healer, though he preferred you… But the spy deserved to die.'

'Why? Do you even know who he was? Do you even know why he was there with the old man?'

'What does it matter? You're always asking questions, Luca. You can never just accept the way things are.'

'It matters because he was not a spy for the Calchwynedd, he was a friend of Veryan Hen's… and our mother's.'

He looks up at me.

'You lie!' He spits gritty mud from his teeth. 'How do you know?'

'His name is… *was* the Jay. He's been coming to Framlutum for years to see me. He was my father.' Despite the mud on his face, I see his eyebrows draw in with confusion. 'Our mother was not always just a potter's wife in an insignificant village. She had a fine life at court and a finer future awaiting her, until it all went wrong and our grandfather was killed.'

'How is it you know so much?'

'I asked her and she told me. You never thought to ask. To you she was just your mother and no more.'

'Because she loved you more!' The hurt twists his mouth into an ugly shape. 'Why did you get to be the one to go to the monastery? She only arranged that you should go – to be like our grandfather, but he was my grandfather too. Why did *I* not get a chance?'

'You never wanted to go! You always ridiculed my learning.'

'I *did* want to go. Of course, I wanted to learn and have a chance to serve the king.'

'It was *King Aurelius* that made the promise, before Mother even came to Framlutum. Anyway, Lucanus would never have allowed it – you were always to inherit the pottery.'

'I've never wanted to be a *potter*,' he spits out mud and wipes his mouth with the cleanest part of his arm. 'Just GO AWAY.' His teeth show white against the mud.

**

I have measured the time passing by the rising tide and the arc of the sun. I have sat on a warm boulder, watching the clouds and the birds that drift carefree and gracefully by. Between the arguments and struggles to get free, Kennan has been still and silent, locked and slowly sinking further in to his fate.

Now, he is up to his armpits. This prolonged entrapment is cruel, torturous, and the awaited death is appalling. I would not be in his shoes. A slight breeze lifts the edge of his hair.

'Luca.' His voice has changed. 'I smell the salt!' He is looking seaward.

'I smell it too. The water is near, not far from the weed line. Once over that, it will flow onto this plain and swirl around your shoulders and the sucking hole that traps you. And you will drown.'

'And you will still be here to watch?' He looks at the mud on his hands. They will never be clean again.

I stand up and take a careful step towards him. My boot soles crunch into the stony edge of the shore.

'LUCA, if you have waited to save me, do it now,' he shouts. 'If you'll not, then GO and leave me to die.'

He is panicking. I see it though he tries not to show it. Even when facing death. That is something I will say for my brother, he is brave. The water is lapping at the weed line. When it rises to his chin, perhaps then he will beg me to save him. Perhaps *then* I will feel the mercy required to pull him free.

'I'm still making my mind up. I owe it to our mother to consider it carefully.'

'You talk as if you are blameless! You tried to kill our father, *my* father. You have done things I can never forgive.'

'Nor I you. Yet still…'

'Go AWAY, Luca.' He slaps at the mud, and it splatters towards me.

'I've been re-living it all and, I cannot deny, there was once *something* between us as brothers. Some small moments of good.'

'They are long buried, and will die with me in this mud.' He twists, trying to turn his back to the shore, to me.

**

The sun has sunk lower and the river water reflects the wider sky. The tide creeps to black weeds. Veryan Hen once asked me if I ever thought that an enemy might turn out not to be an enemy at all. When he saved his enemy from the sea monster, he did so out of an instinctive compassion. It had nothing to do with how worthy the man was, or what future might result from it. Despite their enmity, he was a man Veryan Hen did not really know, a stranger, who became a friend, a sword-brother. For me and Kennan it is quite the reverse. There is no instinctive compassion for the person I know better than any other, I know his faults and his strengths like my own.

His faults and strengths are like my own.

Realisation walks up my spine and creeps over me; I see now what the old man was trying to show me. He gave me the answer years ago. The *real* enemy is Ceawlin. The world is larger than just Framlutum and the petty squabbles of siblings. I have been so focussed on Kennan when I should have been learning how to fight the greatest enemy our people have ever known.

A thread of compassion *is* slowly unwinding.

A softening of understanding that was not there this morning.

'Behind every enemy is a story,' the old man had also said a long time ago. I have told my own story to myself and glimpsed Kennan's story within it. My faults stand out to me now. My perpetual anger gave me a stubborn certainty that Kennan is to blame for all I have lost. But others have affected us more than I realised, there is blame in *many* directions.

It is true, our mother found it hard to show Kennan the same easy love she did me. It is Lucanus who created the initial rivalry between us that has been reinforced over the years by others. Minura, her innocent anger at his unfair treatment made her side with me, rejecting Kennan – Kennan's jealousy made him hurt her which just fanned the flames between us brothers. Bellicia, he liked her first. She played with his attentions. And Vannii, how much of our fights and differences were escalated by him? A poisonous snake adding venom to every dispute. Now poisoned himself.

The things that set me apart in the village, are things that increased his jealousy of me. Veryan Hen – it was not Kennan he told his stories to, or the secrets of healing. Father Faustus, patiently imparting his knowledge, and even the relic, to *me* and not him. My future was intended to be in Glevum serving a king, his was to inherit a pottery he cared nothing for. It was my pot that Prince Coinmail liked, King Aurelius himself singled me out and gave me a coin. Kennan had to bring soldiers and death to gain his.

Kennan has been insensitive, selfish, and aggressive in his reactions to the events of our lives. His actions caused damage that I cannot forgive – but I see now it was not always wilful, deliberate or planned. It was my arrow that killed his dog, though I did not intend it. These things cannot be changed or undone. But if I save him, might it change our lives to come?

I relax my tight fist for the first time in hours. The sun catches the light on the creeping waters, lifting the black weeds and sending its scent of salt. I step closer to the mud. The crunch underfoot makes Kennan look up. He is weak now.

'Give me your hand.'

'Luca, just leave me. I've hated you so long I cannot take your hand now.'

'Give me your hand.'

'Why have you waited 'til now to save me? 'Til it's almost too late?'

He is so weary. I picture him when he was eight, defensive and hurt after Lucanus beat him in the pottery. His eyes have not changed so much, the sad child I wanted to comfort back then is still there within him.

'I'm sorry I did not help you sooner. But I could not.'

'You've watched me struggle for hours, awaiting my death, tormenting me with your presence. Why, only now, do you help me?

Now, when I am at the edge of my death.'

'I wanted you to die, it's true. But not like this.' There is only room for truth here. I must find the words to explain.

'I will get free.' He begins to thrash about desperately. 'WITHOUT your help,' he shouts but his voice cracks, lacking strength. Mud flicks over me. I think back to that play-fight in the clay pits when we were so young. My anger has deserted me and I want to cry.

'Kennan just take my hand.' He appears to sink further. The water has breached the weed line and it cannot be long. 'You remember how we fought the Andeferas boys in Glevum? How we talked of going to war? Our enemies are real and they are *not* you and I. Quickly now, give me your hand. The boy Ceawlin, that prince of the Gewisse, is our enemy. We should not be fighting each other. We have a chance to change things. Take my hand.'

'You know, when we were small, I wanted to be like you, in your quiet way you were everything I wasn't. But then you began to challenge me and make me look foolish. Then you ignored me or argued. I just wanted you to like me.'

'I wanted the same from Lucanus and ended up hating him.' So, I had done to him what Lucanus had done to me. I have the unpleasant taste of remorse. 'Just give me your hand – *now! Hurry!*'

'Luca, I've wanted to kill you so many times. It's not right that you save me – I still hate you.'

'Just *give me your hand*, the sea is coming!'

The long-awaited roll of brown water is spreading across the mud plain.

The black weeds travelling fast towards us.

He finally holds out his hand. I dare not step too close. We stretch to reach each other. Fingertips touch and link. In a firm clasp, I take on the force of suction and pull him, slowly, very slowly he is moving. I think of Veryan Hen pulling his enemy from the teeth of the shark and I know I am doing the right thing.

'Don't let go.'

He is nearing me, just a little, a gap is opening behind him.

The tidal surge of sea and silt crashes into him, pushing him to me as it fills the space at his back. Our hands slip as he gasps at the cold, at the fear. Water bubbles all around. Our grasping hands clasp again, this time with a more secure grip. I pull.

The river that would devour him has finally come but now, along with the force of my pull, it eases the suction and helps to free him. Slowly, he is rising, my weight is counterbalancing. But my feet are sinking. Cold water swirls around, seeping through my boots, churning around his shoulders.

I let go and turn away to grab a large rock.

'Luca, you took everything I loved.'

Does he think I am leaving him?

'Mother, Minura, Bellicia, they all chose you over me. And Redak, you killed her...'

I roll the rock over towards him and push it into the water where my feet were. The tide is lapping his chin. 'Just take my hand again. There's no time to argue. We can't change the past, you said so yourself once, but I'm here now, I'm helping you.'

'You say Ceawlin is our enemy, we have a chance to change the past – but you threw away the relic, Luca. Our only hope!'

Our hands clasp, a death grip. 'It was a false hope,' I say through my teeth as I pull him, my feet firm on the rock. 'The relic brought nothing but division and trouble, even between you and I.' His head rises clear, his other shoulder emerging.

He jerks towards me in the release of the suction. The water fills the space he leaves with a gurgle, and surges around my knees. Our grip is sure, he slides free. The rising water lifts him, his other hand swings up to me.

It holds a knife.

I almost fall back. 'Kennan...' His fist tight in mine, pulling me to him as his other hand slashes at me. I feel the sting in my arm and my chest through the cold swirling water.

'Stop... It doesn't have to be like this.' I wrench my hand from him, struggling to get up.

I stagger toward the shore. He grabs my leg and pulls me back. I fall. A sting on my calf as the knife meets my flesh. I remember when I beat him with the willow stick.

'Kennan, we can *change* the way things are... We can make a new destiny.' Crawling and splashing in the shallows, he stabs at me, over and over. 'Kennan, don't do this.' His face is an ugly crease of loathing. His eyes are screwed against my words.

Red blood blooms in the brown water. I can take no more.

Kicking and thrashing, I rise. I pin him down, my weight on his chest. I want to stop all this, just as I did once before when I held his head in the water. His legs flailing wildly, he strains to keep his head up. Our faces so close, the surface of sea laps between our chins. His arm trapped between us, his knife at my throat.

I feel that tip, nudging and stinging under my chin.

He coughs brown spittle. 'I will send you to the *devil*, Luca.'

My fist over his, muddy and wet. The sting of the knife lancing the softness under my chin. I cannot speak.

The burn of anger fills into my fingers. With two hands against his one, I turn the knife towards him. 'Just *stop* fighting me. Just *stop*.'

'I'll never stop.' He spits water again. 'Not 'til you're dead.'

He collapses back, his head in the water, just the tip of his nose showing. Then his head jerks up to gulp air. He is choking in muddy water. I press my hands down, the knife obscured, submerged but firm, with the tip now at *his* neck.

I hold still. 'It shouldn't end like this.'

In a final effort to gasp air, he surges right up onto the knife at his neck. My muscles are rigid. Frozen in the cold water. The tarnished grey blade with a bright silver edge newly sharpened, pierces the dirty skin beneath his ear, halfway to the hilt.

There is no going back from this moment, no truce to be had, no moving on with the past behind us. He has fought me to the end, he still fights as his body jerks under me. As if turned to stone, I cannot move. Beneath me he writhes and the knife slips further. My fist over his, muddy and wet.

A red cloud in the water.

**

I feel the collapse of resistance. His hand falls away. Water washes over him and he almost disappears from view. I feel the collapse of my own resistance, the tension in every muscle begins to tremble. Rolling off him, I sit with the water lapping around me. The tide will not stop for us. It continues its stealthy rising. My blood mingles with Kennan's, but all I see is the bright wide reflection of sky before me, and the bright wide sky above. His body moves gently as the tide takes him from me.

THE END

Further Stories:

If you enjoyed this story world and would like a little more, I have 5 short illustrated tales on YouTube, just 5 minutes each – search for *Tales of the 6th Century* and you will find:

A Fish Tale (featuring Madoc)

The three Princes of the Dobunni (the end of the life of King Aurelius)

Secrets and Lies (featuring Luca's mother when she is young)

Unbinding Curses (characters from a novel in writing)

The Weight of Words (featuring Father Faustus before he came to Luca's village)

Author's Note on the History

The 6th century is an intriguing time of upheaval and change; by the end of the century much will have been lost and a whole new era begun. Written accounts from this time are contradictory, confusing and unreliable, which is both frustrating and liberating for the storyteller.

The land was divided into tribal regions, re-emerging from pre-Roman identities and with a Brittonic culture that was strong in the west, while Germanic people (Angles, Saxons and Jutes) were settling in the east. Archaeology is uncovering a more mixed population than has been traditionally thought, whether peaceful or violent; what was happening in one area may be different to another, and different again from one decade to the next. It was a time of fast-changing kingdoms, culture and language.

The Roman Empire was long gone although physical remnants of this lost world remained. Old statues and mosaics, crumbling villas and town houses would be part of the fabric of life – walls and fortifications were built to last. Less certain is the Roman cultural influence on ordinary folk. We know it held a grip on the literate and the elite: Gildas, a monk writing at the time, shows an understanding of Roman history and administration. His sophisticated literacy gives an insight into the early Christian Church and its reach – or lack of it. He paints the rulers as godless tyrants and sinners. He outlines the wars against the heathens (Germanic people) but the true picture of this *migration/conquest* is much debated. Gildas was a passionate and opinionated monk with a pious agenda and, as such, is an unreliable source. I can't help but like him, and my character of Father Faustus is drawn heavily from him.

Cerdic is a mystery. The Anglo-Saxon Chronicle (written during the reign of King Alfred in the 9th century), tells us Wessex was founded by Cerdic, who arrived in Hampshire in five ships with his son Cynric in 495, and fought the Britons. It lists victories as he expands his territory around the New Forest, Hampshire and the Isle of Wight, including defeating Natanleod in 508. Then in 519 he *'obtains the kingdom of the West Saxons'*. But, Bede (a monk writing in 8th century) says the name 'West Saxons' arose later – 7th/8th century, though being previously known as the Gewisse (who are, confusingly, thought to have been settlers of the Thames Valley from 5th century). Bede also tells us the Jutes settled in the Meon valley of Hampshire, referring to the area as *'Ytene'* or *'Jutarnum Natio'* – the kingdom of the Jutes; archaeology supports this from early 5th century.

Anglo-Saxon Chronicle entries for the 5th/6th centuries are sketchy, and Cerdic's story is problematic: 1. The Jutes already occupied some of his territory, perhaps even having their own kingdom. 2. Wessex did not exist as a name until the 7/8th century. 3. The name Cerdic is likely to be of Brythonic origin.

Some historians think the landing in five ships and defeating the locals may be a standard Saxon foundation myth and, if Cerdic existed at all, he was not a Saxon. Wessex needed a plausible origin story to give authority over other Anglo-Saxon realms, and maybe Cerdic was a legendary figure to link to. Archaeology shows Britons still lived there, though they do not seem to have retained a group identity into the 6th century. A British nobleman might use Germanic mercenaries (the descendants of the *foederati* hired to guard the Saxon Shore against Pictish raiders) or connections through marriage to wield power. To rule a mixed kingdom successfully, he must have been very charismatic or ruthless. If Cerdic was indeed a king, what was the name of his kingdom? I have called it Jutarnum, and made him king of the Jutes, but this is stretching possibilities rather a lot!

Cynric and Ceawlin are also mysterious kings with Brythonic names. Cynric succeeded Cerdic and was victorious in the battle of Sarum 552, then Barbary Castle, Swindon (Beran Byrg) in 556, pushing his activity further inland. Curiously, this means Cynric fought in battles for over 60 years! He was then succeeded by Ceawlin in 560, active in the Thames Valley area and beyond, and more logically a king of the Gewisse. He was given the title Bretwalda (High King) and by the end of the 6th century, his territory covered an area more consistent with Bede's description of Wessex. His dominance was certainly bad news for the Dobunni, who do not survive beyond the end of the century.

With gaps in the record of Dobunni kingship, I have used a king mentioned by Gildas, one of four he disparages for their sinful ways – Aurelius Caninus (possibly king of the Silures *or* Dobunni). Gildas respected the earlier Ambrosius Aurelianus (late 5th century), of Roman stock whose *parents wore the purple and were slain in it*, a man he portrays as an exceptional leader, whose obedience to God gave him victory at Mons Badonicus (possibly the last great victory over the Saxons). With this in mind, I have given my Aurelius an ambition to match Ambrosius. But all we know is the defeats listed in the Anglo-Saxon Chronicle and what follows them is unclear. The entry for 577 names three kings, Coinmail, Condidan, and Farinmail and the towns Gloucester (Glevum), Cirencester (Corinium) and Bath (Badon), but I will say no more as that is for another story!

Although we cannot take Gildas too literally, he sets a tone for the religious fervour which I wanted to capture – so I invented the search for the lost relics of St Alban. He recounted the story to show a man of faith could convert his executioner from *a wolf to a lamb*. Bede adds that Germinus (a famous visiting bishop) visited the tomb of St Alban, leaving relics of the apostles and other martyrs as gifts, and taking a portion of the earth where the saint's blood was shed. Then on his second visit, he baptised many Britons and led an army to victory, with prayers to the *blessed martyr Alban*. St Alban is mentioned in various texts from the continent through the ages. The town, a place of pilgrimage, retained his name and marks the strength of his renown.

St Albans is in the territory of the Iron Age Catuvellauni tribe, whose region and name changed variously over time, I have used Calchwynedd in the story. By the mid-6th century, they are isolated and surrounded as Saxons have settled the upper Thames, the Chilterns, Essex, and Surrey, with the Angles established in East Anglia and Cambridgeshire, although they continue to hold out into 7th century. King Cadrawd ruled *c*.540-570, but we know little about him.

Another Iron Age tribe that failed to retain its identity is the Atrebates. Their pre-Roman territory was extensive, covering much of central southern England. Archaeology shows Britons were still living there in post-Roman times, but no record of activity exists – perhaps they were conquered or, leaderless and unorganised, they simply lived alongside the Saxons. Any peaceful existence would have ended with the battles of 552 and 556. The old Roman town of Calleva Atrebatum had fallen into decline and was finally abandoned in the 6th century, but curiously the site was never developed and even today the walls remain.

The Dumnonia tribal politics have their own complications, absorbing the Durotriges into their power, but there is no recorded conflict with the Saxons at this time; likewise for the tribes of the Cymru (Wales today). I have brought Brochfael of the Tusks from Powys into my story simply because he is interesting to me and to show a sense of stability among Britons that is not felt by those sharing borders with the Germanic rulers that are dominating.

There is no limit to story potential of 6th-century Britain. Look out for the next book from Lea Moran.

ABOUT THE AUTHOR

Lea Moran

Carer for the elderly

Ex-boatbuilder, window maker, furniture restorer and Celtic giftware artist

Mother of boys

Obsessive history reader

Amateur archaeologist

Part time writer and illustrator

Printed in Poland
by Amazon Fulfillment
Poland Sp. z o.o., Wrocław
14 July 2023

a27a4ac8-1973-4f7b-b94a-33ef3eeb7da2R01